The Mystery Tribe of Camp Blackeagle

The Mystery Tribe of Camp Blackeagle

SIGMUND BROUWER

VICTOR BOOKS
A DIVISION OF SCRIPTURE PRESS PUBLICATIONS INC.
USA CANADA ENGLAND

THE ACCIDENTAL DETECTIVE SERIES

Lost Beneath Manhattan	*Creature of the Mists*
The Mystery Tribe of Camp Blackeagle	*Race for the Park Street Treasure*
Phantom Outlaw at Wolf Creek	*The Downtown Desperadoes*
The Disappearing Jewel of Madagascar	*Madness at Moonshiner's Bay*
The Missing Map of Pirate's Haven	*Sunrise at the Mayan Temple*

Cover illustration by Suzanne Garnier
Ralphy's poems by R.L. Vander Lind

Library of Congress Cataloging-in-Publication Data

Brouwer, Sigmund, 1959–
   The mystery tribe of Camp Blackeagle / by Sigmund Brouwer.
      p.   cm. — (The Accidental detectives series; #2)
   Summary: Spending the summer at cadet camp, Ricky solves the mystery of the Indian spirits and discovers that God's creation is special and deserving of respect.
   ISBN: 0-89693-535-3
   [1. Mystery and detective stories. 2. Camps—Fiction. 3. Christian life—Fiction.]
I. Title.   II. Series: Brouwer, Sigmund, 1959– Accidental detectives series: #2.
PZ7.B79984My   1990
[Fic]—dc20   90-50132
                                                        CIP
                                                          AC

7 8 9 10 11 12 13 14 Printing/Year 97 96 95

VICTOR BOOKS
A division of SP Publications, Inc.
Wheaton, Illinois 60187

With love
to Elizabeth Page

Thank you to the Film and Literary Arts branch
of Alberta Culture and Multiculturism for kind
support provided through a writing grant.

5352

It was the middle of the summer, and I was ready to go crazy. The streets of Jamesville seemed quieter every day, the fish in the creek had stopped biting, and Mike Andrews, my best friend, was at his uncle's farm. Worse, Mike had forgotten to give me my treasure map before he left.

Without the treasure map I was in trouble. One day the week before, we were so bored that we exchanged treasures. Mike gave me his favorite fishing hook, two dollars in dimes, a one-dollar bill, and the baseball card that Steve Garvey's cousin from Three Rivers had signed for a quarter. I gave him a mystery book I was dying to read, four new comic books, and my allowance for the next month. The idea was to bury the other person's treasure and later give him a map to find it.

My Cadet cap was buried too. Cadets is the name of my boys church group, and the cap is part of our uniform. My brother, Joel, was always stealing the cap and using it as a bed for his teddy bear. With summer camp for us Cadets coming up soon, I didn't dare lose the hat, and I figured the cap was more safe buried than not.

Good luck, Ricky Kidd, I told myself. *If you haven't found it by now, you don't have much hope.*

Over the last week, I had nearly been killed by the Bradleys' dogs, the meanest pair of German shepherds to ever get squirted by a water pistol. I thought for sure Mike would have buried it near them. I also had been yelled at by Old Man Jacobsen every time I went near his flower patch. He knew that a shovel in my hand did not mean weeding.

During the week, I had also been scared out of my shoes by Joel three times as he followed and spied on me. I was going crazy from nothing to do, and going crazy thinking about how dumb I was to let someone bury the mystery book I couldn't read and the allowance I couldn't spend. It was so bad, in the morning I almost volunteered to cut our lawn a day early, and barely stopped my mouth in time.

All I had to keep myself from going completely crazy was the thought of Cadet Camp. In three days, the day after Mike got back from the farm, all of us Cadets in the Jamesville area were going into the deep woods way north of Three Rivers for the week-long camp.

To keep myself from doing anything else silly, like visiting Old Man Jacobsen and listening to his army stories, I lay back in the grass of our yard and thought of all the things I would do during that week. I had read everything I could about survival in the deep woods, and I had saved a month's worth of paper route money to buy a hatchet and knapsack.

It was named Camp Blackeagle after a tribe of Indians that used to live along the lake there for centuries. I knew that because Mrs. Hall, our librarian, had found a book on the area for me, and I had read it through three times, especially the part about Indian legends.

I closed my eyes and imagined myself saving the camp counselors from a snarling bear, or being the one to lead everyone back to camp after being lost for days. What an adventure camp would be.

Oh, yes, one week in the woods, and one week without Joel popping out of nowhere to scare me into a heart attack.

As a brother he's OK, I guess. He's only six, and I'm twelve years old and stronger and bigger and everything, but he has his ways of terrifying me. He's like having a personal ghost who shows up at all the worst times.

Joel never says much when you do manage to spot him. He just stares and watches. It seems he can get through locked doors and closed windows. He disappears as soon as you turn your head, and appears again when you least expect it. Which is usually when you're doing something you shouldn't. Those are the times I faint or have heart attacks. Or fall into disaster.

It figured that just as I thought of Joel, his shadow would cross my face. I hadn't heard him approach—he's quieter than growing grass—but I knew all I had to do was open my eyes, and there he'd be, staring mournfully at me.

The shadow passed, which meant he wasn't staying, which meant something was up.

I bolted upright, and managed to grab the back of his pants before he reached the shed. Once he's out of sight for half a second, he's gone like smoke on a windy day.

Sure enough, in his arms he had his teddy bear wrapped in my Cadet cap. I took the cap from him and slapped it back into straightness against my leg. Joel smiled and walked away.

The smile hit me. My Cadet cap! He knew where my treasure was buried!

I ran, but didn't bother shouting because he never listened anyway. By the time I rounded the corner of the shed, it was too late. He was gone.

It was time to go to a bigger power.

I marched into the kitchen to tell Mom exactly what her

second-born son had managed to do. She was listening to the telephone with a worried look on her face. She waved me quiet and listened carefully.

"OK," she said, "We'll be there in three days. I'm glad it wasn't worse."

When she hung up, she took a deep breath to talk to me. That wasn't a good sign. She put her hands on my shoulders. A worse sign.

"Ricky, that was your Aunt Trudy. She broke a leg falling down her porch steps. It looks like your father and I are going to have to go there for a week or so until things settle down for her."

That wasn't so bad. Sometimes a serious talk means I'm in big trouble. I started to tell her about Joel and the buried treasure.

"Just a second," she said. "I have to make another call."

When the other person answered, she said, "Hello, Mr. Vanderhoek, I'm calling because my sister who lives out of town broke her leg and needs help."

There was a pause. "No, Mr. Vanderhoek, she didn't ask for your help."

I grinned because I could picture his face scrunched with thought as he considered why Aunt Trudy might ask him for help. He is the head of the boys church group, and nothing ruffles him. Mr. Vanderhoek thinks everything through and always speaks carefully and slowly, and he doesn't think of you as a kid. He is the kind of Christian I would like to be. He also smiles a lot when he's not thinking.

"I'm calling about the summer camp," my mom said.

Hold on, I thought, *Aunt Trudy doesn't need me, even if I do have my first-aid badge.*

"Yes, Ricky's still going to camp," she said after pausing to hear Mr. Vanderhoek's question.

Whew.

She continued. "Unfortunately, Ricky's father needs to go with me. Since my sister has three kids and barely any extra room in her house, I'm calling to see if you can make an exception to let an under-age camper go to camp."

When my mom uses that tone, it's impossible to say no. I wasn't surprised to hear her say thank-you before hanging up. I wondered which of my cousins they were sending to camp to meet me.

"I'm glad that worked out," she said. "Now your father and I can go help Aunt Trudy while you look after Joel and enjoy summer camp together." She paused. "What was that you came busting in the kitchen to tell me?"

I nearly fainted. Joel nearby in the deep woods? I barely survived him here in Jamesville. She couldn't be serious about sending him to camp.

She snapped me out of my daze by repeating her question. "What did you rush in to say, Ricky?"

"Nothing," I said with resignation. "Nothing important anymore."

I had to begin emergency preparations right away.

It was Saturday morning, two days before camp. Mike wouldn't be back from his uncle's farm until late Sunday afternoon, and by then it would be too late for his map to help. I needed my buried allowance money *before* Sunday to be able to hit the stores and assemble emergency items for Joel's week at camp.

In other words, I was desperate to find my buried treasure before the day was out. The frightening part was that only Joel knew where it was.

At breakfast, I began my plan. "Mom," I said, "it's the craziest thing. I lost my comic book collection earlier this week, but I suddenly remember exactly where I left it."

Joel stopped crunching on his cereal.

"Is it OK if I get it before I cut the lawn?" Saturday mornings were yardwork times for Joel and me.

She rolled her eyes. "How does someone lose . . . forget I asked. I don't want to know. Go ahead, but remember how hard it is to keep Joel from disappearing before it's time to rake the cuttings."

Joel kept his head down. He's usually quiet, but gets quieter when someone talks about him. Some people think it's strange that Joel doesn't talk much, and when he does, he says as little as possible. I know it's just Joel. He already knows how to read, and even print out complete sentences, and he knows more words than most kids his age. But he's shy, and he mispronounces big words once in a while, so he gets his out-loud sentences over with as fast as he can.

"I know," I said. "Sometimes I feel like burying his teddy bear. Of course, I wouldn't dream of leaving it where I lost my comics."

Dad groaned as he pictured Joel without the teddy bear. "Ricky, your mother is already dealing with her sister's broken leg. We don't need another state of emergency in this household."

Joel squirmed in his chair. The teddy bear is his only weak point. Once Old Man Jacobsen's dog dragged it away, and Joel dug in all the dog's favorite hiding spots with his plastic toy shovel until he found it a couple of hours later. He wouldn't let me help. Even the dog was smart enough to stay out of sight.

Sometimes, when I need to be alone, I put the teddy bear into the dryer. Joel watches it tumble until the cycle ends.

What he didn't know now was that I already had the teddy bear. My timing had to be perfect. When breakfast ended, Joel and I both bolted from the table and headed in opposite directions.

I dashed to the big oak tree on the corner of our street. That vantage point showed most of the avenues of escape from our house. I gave Joel about another 30 seconds.

First, he'd check his room for the bear's hiding spot, which wasn't much of a hiding spot. Joel thinks if the bear's eyes are covered, nobody else can see it.

Then, he'd panic, remembering my threat during breakfast about burying the bear.

Just about now, I guessed, *his legs are churning down the stairs as he scrambles to find me.* With luck, worry would cloud his radar-like sensing ability. Normally, he's impossible to sneak up on.

The screen door is just about to—bingo!—*slam.* Hah! For Joel, making noise like that meant he was really worried.

He zipped past the front of the oak tree at a full run. A hundred yards later, I began to follow him.

It was easy. The little guy had only one thing on his mind. His bear and where it would be buried. He dashed right past Old Man Jacobsen's yard.

He sped past the Bradleys. Naturally, their German shepherds didn't howl at him. Not that I actually expected it. Something about Joel makes animals and birds trust him. When I passed the dogs on tiptoe, they immediately went crazy with barking. Fortunately, Joel was too worried to notice. The run was tiring him, and he had to slow to a trot, but not once did he look back.

When he reached Mrs. Danielson's house, he skidded to a stop. I did too. Mrs. Danielson has a big house with a large front porch. She's been a friend to both of us ever since her husband died and we tried too hard to help her out—but that's another story in itself.

Joel crept onto the grass and inched toward the front steps of the house. Joel must have followed Mike as he buried my treasure before leaving for the farm. If my plan had worked, my comics and money would not be far from him now.

I watched from a distance until he had nearly reached the porch. Of course, the porch! Mike and I both knew it was a great hiding spot.

I practiced my Indian style of quiet walking that I had learned by reading manuals on how to survive in the woods. Joel's radar-sensing ability was clouded all right, because he didn't hear me as I rustled through the grass behind him.

I tapped him on the shoulder and he jumped two feet off the ground.

You would think after all the times he has done exactly the same to me, he would be a good sport, but no. When he landed he sputtered with rage and excitement and didn't calm down until I handed him his teddy bear.

I crouched to look beneath the porch.

There was the creak of an opening door, and I looked up to see Lisa Higgins. How could I forget she spends Saturday mornings cleaning there? I would have preferred dealing with Mrs. Danielson.

Lisa's the kind of girl who drives Mike and me and Ralphy Zee, our other friend, nuts by hitting home runs off our pitching. It hardly makes up for it that she always acts sorry when she beats us on math tests.

"Hi, Ricky. Mrs. Danielson's not home," she said. "I don't think she's under the porch either."

"Hello," I said, still crouched. "Um, Joel and I were wondering if you knew what time it is."

She giggled. "Joel didn't wonder too hard. He's gone."

I looked around. How he does it, I'll never know.

She giggled again. "And I'd tell you the time, except I can't read your wrist-watch from here."

Why can't I ever come up with the right excuses when I need them?

Lisa always catches me doing dumb things. The problem is that she's pretty, so you never know if you should like her as a friend, or what. She has long dark hair that she ties in a ponytail to play baseball, and when she smiles, it's like sunshine breaking through clouds. It's enough to make you try to get her to smile—if she hasn't made you look stupid for a while. Not that I would ever admit it to Mike or Ralphy.

Before I could say anything, she said, "Wait here, Ricky."

She went into the house, so I moved closer to sneak a better look under the porch. I got on my hands and knees to peer under the steps. Sure enough, among the sunshine and shadows that trickled under the porch, I could see footprints and shovel marks. I'd have to come back later.

"Looking for this?" I heard a voice say. I bumped my head scrambling to get up. Lisa giggled again and held out a plastic bag.

"I saw Joel scoot out of there yesterday with his teddy bear wrapped in some crazy looking hat, so I took a look myself," she said. "Glad to see I was right."

"Excuse me?"

"It's insane to bury anything under Mrs. Danielson's porch. So I knew you or Mike were responsible."

Through a big coughing spell, I managed to politely accept the bag. She said, "Don't worry, I didn't take your money."

She giggled some more as my face turned white.

I scrambled through the bag. My nice, fat white envelope with the money was gone. I nearly screamed. Not only a whole week in suspense wondering about it, but finally outsmarting my brother for the first time in years, and still no money. Or comics.

Mike and I had some serious talking to do.

Lisa said, "Flip through your book."

A note. *If you're worried about your money, try your piggy bank. That's where it belongs anyway, you dummy. Your pal, Mike.*

Not a word about my comic books. Lisa said, "Ricky Kidd, you sure are cute when you get frantic."

Wonderful. *Cute* is not the word rugged campers like to hear just before leaving. Good thing Lisa wouldn't be there.

The only reason I could fake a smile at her was because I

thought of how Mike was going to pay for all this as he got *his* treasure back. When the Bradleys took their German shepherds for a walk, I had buried Mike's treasure in the dirt floor of their doghouse.

"Wish me luck," Lisa said.

"Sure. Good luck. Why?"

She smiled. "With you and Mike and Ralphy at camp, some-one's got to rescue Jamesville from Joel."

"Thanks anyway," I said. "But Joel's going to camp too."

Her look of sympathy made me feel like she was saying good-bye to someone about to face a firing squad.

After cutting the lawn, I went to Thompson's grocery store and picked out the emergency supplies I needed. For once, Joel didn't follow me. He was still upset at being fooled.

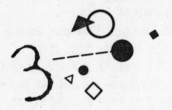

"OK, Mike, where are my comic books?" I said.

"Come on, I'm barely awake." We were standing in the parking lot waiting for the bus to arrive. Mike looked funny with his red hair sticking out in all directions.

I happen to think he looks a little funny most of the time, but he's bigger than I am and there's no sense in testing a friendship by seeing who might win a fight. Mike's got this rule about sneakers—they can't match. His left shoe is always a different color than his right shoe, and he has more pairs to choose from than I have comic books. I just wish sometimes the shoes would match the colors of his Hawaiian shirts. When he whizzes by on a skateboard, it hurts my eyes to watch him.

It was seven o'clock Monday morning.

"Barely awake," I said. "Give me a break. I've been waiting twenty minutes, and you were here before me."

He shrugged.

"Four comic books," I said, pushing four fingers near his face. "No treasure map, and four comic books missing. Explain that or suffer the consequences."

"I think the counselors have forgotten this is the week for camp. Where are they?" He looked in all directions, shielding his eyes from the sun like an experienced camper.

"Mr. Vanderhoek is probably still trying to wake up Ted." Ted Weibe was one of the younger counselors; we all knew he loved sleeping. Once the counselors had taken us to an educational movie on African animals. When we left, Ted was still in the front row, snoring away.

Besides Ted and Mr. Vanderhoek, the other counselors for the week were Charlie Waisely and Bud James. We liked all four of them. But it never took us long on these outings to remember we didn't like their cooking.

Mike kept looking around with his eyes shielded.

"Hold on, Pal," I said. His trick would not work. "They'll get here when they get here. What about my comic books?"

"You won't believe me anyway."

"Try me." Then I shouted, "Joel, get back here." As usual, he was barely visible, searching around in the grass for anything of interest.

"I borrowed them," Mike said.

I tried to be patient. "Mike, I borrow your things too and don't always tell you until after, but I do return them."

"Your uncle doesn't have a farm and friends like Billy One and Billy Two."

"My uncle doesn't have a crummy nephew like you either, does he?"

"Both Billies really liked your comics."

"Joel, get back here before you get dirty!" When I realized what I was saying, I groaned. Dirt would be the least of my worries with him for a week. Worse, I was sounding like a mother.

Mike was grinning at me.

"Comic books right now!" I shouted.

He shouted back. "I can't give them to you because two of my uncle's goats ate them!"

"Goats?" I kept shouting.

"Yes, Billy One and Billy Two!" He tried shouting over me, but as I got mad he started laughing and nearly choked. So he reached into his knapsack and threw down the remnants of four comic books. They were scrunched almost into balls and the ink had run and then faded.

Mike took advantage of my stunned disbelief and started running.

What saved him was the arrival of our counselors in the rackety yellow bus they had borrowed from our school. I had to switch attention to finding Joel.

By the time I corralled him, the rest of the guys were in the bus, Mike had returned and wiped off most of his grin, and I had calmed down.

"Billy goats," I muttered as we climbed up the steps together. "Just have fun getting your own buried treasure back."

As usual, there was a bit of pushing and shoving as all of us decided where to sit. The counselors waited patiently. They knew it was better for us to settle down now than take half the trip doing it.

It was hard to decide. If you sat in the front, you could see where you were going and ask the counselors questions. If you sat in the back, you could be a little louder without making the counselors mad, or you could discuss secret plans. The window seat was great because you could have the breeze and watch scenery. On previous trips, for a while, the counselors had allowed us to stick our arms out and wave them in the rushing air, until Ralphy Zee had been hit by a bumblebee once. Which wasn't good, because Ralphy is excitable and he made a lot of noise.

However, the window seat also had a drawback. You could get

sandwiched. The way it worked was that a bunch of us would sneak up the aisle and cram into the seat and sandwich the window person against the side of the bus. One time when it happened to Mike, it squished the banana inside his shirt. But that's what he got for not sharing.

Mr. Vanderhoek stood up at the front of the bus.

"The first thing I want to say is all of us should pitch in and buy a certain someone an alarm clock."

A mixture of cheers and boos were sent in Counselor Ted's direction.

"The second thing I want to say is we have a young guest among us. I'm sure you all know him. He is Ricky's younger brother, Joel."

Mike punched my arm. Ralphy patted Joel on the back. Joel stared at his knapsack which was on the floor at his feet. Everybody else remembered the last school program when Joel was the back end of a donkey during a play and his efforts made it a disaster.

Mr. Vanderhoek continued. "Joel is here because his parents had to attend to a family emergency. He is not only in my care and Ricky's care, but all of our care. Remember that."

Most of the Cadets nodded. Mike punched my arm again. I shook my head sadly. I figured Joel needed as much care as a fox, and that I would be lucky to last a week with him showing up from nowhere every five minutes.

"It will be about six hours by bus to camp. Try to behave like sane human beings for at least half of that time. And if anyone asks 'how much further' or says they have to go to the bathroom, they will peel potatoes for a week."

He smiled his nice smile and we all knew he was enjoying himself.

"Now," he said, "all of us are in God's care. Let's ask Him to continue watching over us during this week, and thank Him for giving us this chance to be together."

We were all quiet during the prayer. When he finished, there was some more quiet, then the bus lurched forward.

We all cheered.

●

It took sixty miles for the first person to get sandwiched. We were headed north, driving along a road that followed the Crow River, which ran through Jamesville. It met two other small rivers near the town of Three Rivers.

It was a nice drive, even for a group of Cadets busting to be at camp as soon as possible. The valleys had trees and pastures and fields of wheat, and it seemed peaceful.

That peacefulness fooled Ralphy.

Not that Ralphy is hard to fool. He is a computer whiz, but he can lose track of things that happen around him when he's away from the screen. In fact, he sometimes needs protecting, which was the job that belonged to Mike and me. Of course, with friends the occasional joke makes things interesting.

So Mike and I crept along the aisle, pretending we had to talk to someone at the back of the bus. We bolted into Ralphy's seat and started squishing. More jumped in. It seemed like about fifteen of us were crowding into Ralphy's seat. He squealed and giggled and promised to get all of us back. We weren't doing too well either, because like dummies we were at the front of the sandwich, with about fourteen people squishing us.

Mr. Vanderhoek walked to the back of the bus.

He held his watch in front of him and began counting down. "Fifteen, fourteen, thirteen, twelve..." The unofficial rules were a maximum of twenty seconds of full squish. Any more and strange duties would be imposed on us at camp. The counselors had good imaginations, so we never tested them more than a few times each year.

"... Eight, seven, six, five, four, three, two, one, and stop."

"Good one," Ralphy said when he could breathe again. "Better me than Joel."

Nothing to make you feel worse than someone actually turning the other cheek.

"I wouldn't worry about him getting it," Mike said. "Joel being Joel, he's already got a plan in case anyone tries it on him."

As I looked around the bus, I saw only two guys who might actually pick on a six-year-old kid. Jim and Bruce Martin. They were twins, and always agreed with each other. They didn't mind doing everything possible to win, either, like the time they put Crazy Glue on Ralphy's bat handle, and he spent so much time trying to drop it that by the time he got to first base he was out by miles.

If they started something, it would put any other big brother in an awkward position. You feel bad if you don't protect your little brother, but you don't want to protect him so much he never learns to stand on his own. Not me. I know too well how terrifying Joel can be. His only weak point was his teddy bear, and his teddy bear was the only area I would get fighting mad for him.

* * * * * * * *

When we stopped for a picnic break, I confiscated Joel's

teddy bear before he could leave his seat. It was my only insurance we wouldn't need a search party later.

We tumbled out of the bus. Joel, of course, disappeared. I should have suspected something because he didn't even stop to eat.

My only regret during that lunch was knowing that my mushed peanut butter and jelly sandwich was still ten times better than anything I could expect from the counselors over the next week.

It seemed like barely any time passed before it was time to go back onto the bus. "Joel!" I yelled. "Time to throw away your teddy bear!"

There was a rustling in the bushes beside the bus, and Joel stepped through, staring mournfully at me.

My suspicion should have grown when he walked onto the bus holding his jacket in front of him, instead of taking his teddy bear from me like usual.

The next sandwich happened when Ralphy was squatting in the aisle, talking to me and Mike. That left the space on the bus seat beside Joel open. I noticed a little late that he was wide open to a sandwich attack, though only someone like Jim or Bruce would sandwich a six-year-old.

It didn't take them long. "Now," grunted Jim as they snuck up the aisle.

"Shhh!" said Bruce. About ten others followed, not knowing who was going to be the victim.

From two rows up, we saw every detail of the attack, but it was already too late to help Joel.

Jim and Bruce stood in front of Joel for one second and gloated. It was their biggest mistake. As all of them rammed in for the sandwich, Joel disappeared.

To most people, it looks like magic. In fact, it still looks like magic to me and I have seen him do it hundreds of times. He can be sitting at the dinner table, then swoosh, he relaxes completely and slides straight down quicker than you can blink. By the time you realize where he has gone, he has already crawled out from under the table and vanished.

This time, he took a little longer than usual in disappearing and barely left in time. At first, I thought the cramped bus seat had slowed him down. We soon found out the real reason.

He resurfaced between Mike and me and looked back at the sandwich with us. Jim and Bruce, being the first ones in, were the ones getting squished into the side of the bus. Joel had been with us for less than a second before Jim and Bruce discovered their mistake.

"Yeeooowwwww!" Together they were louder than the Bradleys' German shepherds howling at the moon. Except Jim and Bruce showed more passion.

"Yeeeeeeoooooooowwwwwww!" The others behind them thought Jim and Bruce were trying to be funny, so they started howling too. The bus echoed with it. "Yeeeeeeoooooooowwwwwww!"

Mr. Vanderhoek, who was back there with his watch, counting down the seconds, could barely keep from laughing at the various tones.

He finally shouted above the howling. " . . . Three, two, one, finished!" It's a good thing the sandwich crew heard him, otherwise Jim and Bruce would still be yowling.

I caught a ghost of a smile on Joel's face. Then I knew the yowling wasn't a joke. Jim and Bruce came out of the sandwich hopping and bouncing down the aisle of the bus. They plucked at their sides and arms and legs. "Oooh, aaah!" they said in unison. "Aaah, oooh!"

I went back to look. Part of the evidence was still on the bus seat, the remnants of what Joel had brought onto the bus wrapped in his jacket. The extra time it had taken for him to

disappear under the seat in front of him was the time it took
him to empty the jacket.

Jim and Bruce plucked desperately at themselves.

They had bravely sandwiched an armful of bramble bush and
thorns.

●

As Bruce and Jim plucked at themselves, the open valleys and green pastures with stands of trees gradually gave way to a thick forest with the odd break at rivers, streams, or small lakes. The wide-paved road narrowed, then became a gravel road. We were very close to the campsite.

When we finally stopped again, at a small general store, Jim and Bruce were still picking at themselves and whimpering a little.

The bus lurched to a stop again, and we all piled out. Again I had Joel's teddy bear. This time he took his lunch bag. He had seen lots of stores before, so he wore his knapsack like a proud explorer and prowled the trees and bushes at the edge of the parking lot.

Some of the others stayed outside. Not me. I knew it would be a week before seeing civilization again. The counselors would give us nothing but healthy food, the worst kind. I wanted a chance at one last root beer.

The store was dark inside, with hundreds of dusty items crammed on all the shelves. A bearded man with a red nose and

big belly sat in a rickety chair behind the counter. He got up as
we brought our money out to pay for our stuff.

"Boys," he said, "you must be headed for Camp Blackeagle."
We nodded.

The man leaned forward on the counter and dropped his
voice. "I gotta tell you. There's been some mighty strange happenings out there."

In the darkness of the old store, it was almost frightening the
way he whispered from behind his beard.

"Yup," he said. "Not many people go out there, and the last
group came back early. They stopped in here for some gas, filled
up, and left in a big hurry. Scared, they were."

Ralphy stuttered. "Sc-scared?"

"That's right, boys, scared." The man stepped back again,
looked around, then leaned forward. "They said it were ghosts.
Indian spirits that was haunting them."

A girl stepped out from behind a door at the back of the
store. She had blond hair, shoulder-length and curly. Her blue
jeans were scuffed, and she wore a lumberjack shirt.

"That's my girl there," the man said. "Sheila. She's only
twelve, but helps run this store as good as anybody. In fact,
she'll be delivering your fresh supplies every day."

She stepped forward and stared at us. "If you're going to the
camp, you're in danger," she said. "I'd stay away if I were you."

Mike said, "Ghosts don't scare me."

Was that an angry look she gave us, or was it my imagination?
Her father said, "They sure scared the other campers."

I remembered the book Mrs. Hall gave me.

"Isn't there some legend around here?"

"Yup," he said. "A legend of the Blackeagle massacre. The
way it goes, a couple hundred years ago, the Blackeagle Indians
called a truce to make peace with another tribe. They invited
them to the lake shore for a huge feast and discussions. In the

middle of the night, the other tribe took weapons they had hidden nearby and killed every Blackeagle Indian while they were sleeping. And now they haunt the lake."

Ralphy moved closer to me. I didn't mind.

The man said, "I don't believe it myself, but that makes two groups in a row that's left early. Strange goings on."

Sheila said, "I believe it, and I'd never stay there at night. Especially not in tents."

She stared at us with her angry defiant look until we left the store.

In the bright sunlight, Mr. Vanderhoek laughed. "OK, who believed that?"

Ralphy started putting up his hand, but Mike grabbed it and held it down.

"He probably says that to every new group of campers," I said, trying to be brave.

Mr. Vanderhoek looked at our faces and decided we really were scared. His voice became gentler. "Boys, remember you all have the armor of Paul. No ghost can get through that."

We grinned back. Paul was his favorite New Testament example because he was a fighter, relying on the armor of his Christianity.

We trooped to the bus, anxious to get to camp. Joel hopped aboard, even before I needed to wiggle even a leg of the teddy bear, and sat beside Ralphy. When the bus turned off the gravel road onto a skinny dirt road, Joel scampered to the front to see what was happening. Ralphy was still a bit nervous, so I moved beside him, careful not to step on Joel's knapsack on the floor.

We bumped our way down the dirt road. It was so narrow that branches scraped across the side of the bus. We were quiet with anticipation.

Finally, ahead through the trees, we could see the blue of a lake. We were very close, and everyone cheered. It got quiet again just as we reached the gates that said "Camp Blackeagle."

As we drove through, all of us lost in thoughts about the week ahead, Ralphy stirred beside me.

I congratulated myself on surviving the trip with Joel. Then Ralphy hopped a bit.

"Hang on, Ralphy," I said. "We'll be there in a second."

Without warning, he stood up and screamed at the top of his voice. He jumped up and down on the bus seat and screamed louder, shaking his legs so hard he nearly kicked me. Everybody on the bus froze.

"Aaaaaargh. Heeeeeeelp! Aaaaaaaah!"

Ralphy leaped straight into the air, banged his head on the bus roof, and landed, running, in the aisle of the bus. He reached the door as the bus stopped, rammed it open with his shoulder, and tore straight ahead, jumping and shaking, screaming and yelling. He ran so fast and hard, within seconds he had disappeared in the direction of the lake.

The entire bus was stunned. Before I could move, I felt something brush against my leg. I ignored it. Suddenly, something was wrapped around my entire leg and moving upwards. I leaped up and started shaking my leg.

"Aaaaaargh. Heeeeeeelp! Aaaaaaaah!"

At least I didn't bang my head on the roof of the bus before I hit the aisle in a full run, and tore through the open door.

I ripped along as fast as I could, terrified out of my mind. Whatever had my leg was holding tighter the faster I ran and the harder I shook. I reached Ralphy within a hundred yards, but I was too scared to stop. We looked at each other, screamed, and kept running.

We were so terrified, we didn't even see the water. I hit it first and screamed some more and hopped up and down and fell. Ralphy fell beside me about three seconds later.

We surfaced. I couldn't feel anything on my leg. I looked

down. Ralphy stopped screaming, puzzled. "It's gone," he said.

By then, the counselors reached the lake. They looked plenty worried.

We both jumped again. Two snakes surfaced right beside us and calmly swam in opposite directions.

"Garter snakes," I said in disgust. "Not even Joel is scared of . . ."

I slapped the water and yelled. Ralphy jumped right out of the water. I didn't know how, but it had to be Joel's fault. "Jooooeeeel! I'm getting you for this!"

The counselors nearly rolled into the lake beside us, they laughed so hard. I would get them too.

We had arrived at camp.

6

I was lying in the sun on a big rock by the lake, trying to dry off, as Mike came out of the woods.

"Aren't you supposed to be helping unload the bus?" I asked.

Mike grinned. "Nope. I told them I was going to help Ralphy calm down. Besides, you could be helping unload too."

I sat up and yawned. "Not me. I'm still in shock."

Ralphy was on the other rock, mumbling at the sky and checking his legs every few seconds.

"And Joel's going to be in bigger shock as soon as I dry off," I said.

Mike started laughing. He told me what happened on the bus right after Ralphy and I screamed out of there. Mr. Vanderhoek and Counselor Ted had chased after us, worried sick.

The other counselors had their hands full on the bus. Just when our screams were out of hearing range, everyone else started hopping. There wasn't a place on the bus without snakes wriggling at full speed. Mike said there were Cadets and snakes going in all directions, all wanting off the bus. Except for Joel.

When Counselor Charlie counted Cadets, he didn't see Joel,

so he looked back into the bus. Joel was patiently rounding up snakes and trying to put them back into his knapsack.

It seemed impossible that he could have found dozens of snakes during the short time we were in the store. To all of the Cadets, who had seen what looked like hundreds of snakes flashing in all directions, Joel's powers seemed spooky.

It wasn't until later when I read something in a biology book that I guessed how he had done it. Garter snakes sometimes gather in big bunches, wriggling themselves into a huge ball.

Joel isn't scared of anything. Tickled pink, he must have grabbed the entire bunch and slung them into his knapsack. After bouncing on the floor of the bus, Ralphy's pant leg and mine must have looked like peaceful places, though we proved them wrong in a big hurry.

Only one thing was certain by the time everything calmed down. Joel and his powers for terrifying people had everyone's full attention.

After Mike explained it to me, I knew it was time for emergency preparation number one.

I hopped off the rock. As I left, Mike started telling Ralphy a snake joke.

* * * * * * * *

The camp looked like an exciting place to explore. The trees were not really close together, so there was room to run at full speed. At the edges of the camp area, the bushes closed in again.

The kitchen cabin was in the middle of the camp area. It had windows with screens instead of glass. Inside it were three picnic tables and a huge potbelly stove.

Close by the kitchen cabin was another cabin, a little smaller. It had bunks. This is where the counselors were staying. A line of Cadets carried piles of stuff inside.

I followed the line back to the bus. Sure enough, Mr. Vanderhoek was patiently directing traffic.

Most of the stuff was already unloaded. It was about one o'clock, and the Cadets were busting to start putting up their own tents. Mr. Vanderhoek thought that was fine, as long as the counselors' gear and the kitchen supplies were moved from the bus first.

It took ten minutes of patient watching to spot Joel prowling in the bushes on the other side of the bus and another ten minutes to get close enough to nab him.

"Joel," I said. "This is for your good as well as ours." I took out the first of my emergency preparations, four sets of bells.

Joel sat patiently as I tied them securely to his wrists and ankles. I didn't tie them tightly enough to hurt him, but I pulled the knots so hard that no six-year-old in the world would have been able to undo them.

When I let go of him, he stood slowly and shook himself with dignity. The bells rang loudly. Despite the jangles, he walked away majestically, in the same way the bears do that you see on television after they have been shot with a dart gun and tagged. For a second, I was almost sad, but then I remembered the snakes.

The bus was unloaded, and at the side of the bus, Ralphy, finally able to move without twitching, was now guarding the pile of gear that included our tent.

"About ready, Ralphy?"

He nodded.

Twenty yards away, Jim and Bruce Martin guarded their own pile of gear. They glared at me. Jim sneered. "Nice trick on the bus, Ricky, but next time you won't be there to help your brother be so sneaky."

I shrugged. If they didn't know by now not to mess with Joel, nothing could protect them.

Mike came running up. "Guys, I found the best spot ever for a tent." He looked at Jim and Bruce, then at us again. "Yup, it's got a clear view to the lake and a good breeze so the bugs will leave us alone. Better yet, it's flat, smooth, and hardly needs any clearing. In fact, all I need is a broom."

He hopped onto the bus, and reached behind the driver's seat for the broom we always used to clean the bus after school trips.

"Be right back." He spoke loudly enough for Jim and Bruce to hear. "I'm glad no one else found this spot first."

He trotted in the direction of the lake again. Just before we lost sight of him, he stopped and began sweeping leaves and grass in all directions.

"What's with him?" I said. "Mike usually runs away from anything that looks like work."

"It must be quite a spot," Ralphy said. "Last time Mike got a blister he fainted, remember?"

I snorted. "That faint was no accident. You forget how he got out of working the rest of the day because of it."

Jim and Bruce were watching carefully too. Little did I know what was going through their minds, or Mike's.

The air echoed with the chopping sounds of Cadets clearing away trees. Some of the younger Cadets started hacking away at the large trees, only to quit partway through. Groups all across shouted and laughed at dumb jokes.

Behind me, I heard a jangle of bells. Joel was fifty feet away, heading toward the shade of a large oak tree with half a sandwich in his hand. He stopped and sat. He held out a piece of bread and looked up expectantly. A fat squirrel up a couple of branches in the tree peered downward at him.

The squirrel slowly came down the tree and daintily hopped onto the ground beside Joel. He moved closer, almost to Joel's leg, then jumped back quickly, testing Joel's intentions. Joel stayed still as a rock. The squirrel moved closer again, crouched, waited for half a second, then darted ahead to grab the chunk of bread before running back to the tree.

There was a clang of wood on metal behind me. Mike had thrown the broom back into the bus.

"That's that," he said, dusting his hands off against his pants. "We'll have our tent up in a jiffy. No Cadets could have it easier than us."

Jim and Bruce were still waiting and watching.

Mike slapped his head. "Oh nuts. I forgot we were supposed to help Mr. Vanderhoek. He's in the kitchen piling some wood, and he wants everyone in our tent to help him."

Ralphy protested. "But Mike, what about setting up our tent?"

"It won't go anywhere without us," Mike said. "Besides, that spot makes it so easy to put up a tent we'll make up lost time in a flash."

"But—"

Mike was already moving in the direction of the kitchen. Ralphy followed slowly. I moved last, knowing if Mike was up to something, only patience would show me. I heard the jangling of bells as Joel kept me in sight.

* * * * * * * *

When we got back from the kitchen, Jim and Bruce and their stuff were already at the spot Mike had cleared for our tent. It didn't surprise me, so I stayed quiet.

Ralphy yelped. "I told you, Mike. I knew they'd do that."

As we marched closer, we saw that they already had the base of their tent securely pegged.

Jim spoke first. "Finders, keepers, losers, weepers."

Bruce said, "Yeah. If you don't like it, run and find a counselor. Maybe they'll fight your battles for you."

"Nobody said anything about a fight, so hang on to your drawers," I said. "Mike cleared this spot, and you guys knew it."

Jim smirked. "We thought he changed his mind because he never went back to it."

We waited for Mike to get mad. Instead, he spoke calmly. "It's OK guys, even if this is the spot that *Ricky* told me to clear." What was he up to? I know better than to ask Mike to work.

Mike continued. "We'll find another spot even if this is the one Ricky wanted. Besides, this area is supposed to be haunted, right? Maybe Indian ghosts will pick on Jim and Bruce as punishment."

Everybody laughed at that. We all remembered it later.

"Mike," I asked as we walked back to the bus, "why did you tell Jim and Bruce that the spot was my idea?"

"You're so smart, I knew you'd have picked it if you saw it."

I didn't believe him for a second.

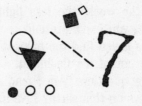

"Mike, who's going to get the dumbest-joke-of-the-week award?"

"Probably Counselor Ted. He'll ask us why the Cadet crossed the road."

Camp was already dark as we walked to the main campfire. Lights bobbed around us like fireflies as all of us went by different routes for the chance to have to use our flashlights.

"Aren't you mad about losing our tent site?" I asked.

Mike swung his flashlight into my eyes. I sighed and pushed the flashlight away.

"Maybe. Maybe not," he said, then used his flashlight beam to carefully examine the branches of the nearest tree. Something about the light of a flashlight makes you look twice at everything you ignore during the day. Mike swung his light down to check out a rock.

No matter how many times you camp, and how many times you tell yourself this is the time you will use your flashlight only when you need to, it goes dead before the third night.

For the first two nights, if something moves in the dark near the campfire, zap, it seems like two hundred flashlights snap on

to point at it. You also shine the flashlight up your nose forty
times, even if everybody else has showed you forty times how
red their nose looks in a flashlight beam. Then, of course, you
have to make big hand shadows on your tent wall for at least
half an hour or until Ralphy gets too scared to take it anymore.

The longer into the week, the less light bobbing there is.
With dead batteries, you can't pretend to be brave and walk
alone. What happens is you find the nearest person with even a
faint yellow coming out of his flashlight.

Mike answered my question. "Am I mad about the tent site?
Aren't we all brothers on this earth? Live and let live, I always
say. Virtue is its own reward."

Why didn't I believe *that* story?

He ignored me to hum tunelessly and check the shadows that
his flashlight made on roots sticking out of the ground. Behind
us, the jangles of Joel's bells followed.

We reached the campfire. The counselors had found a couple
of thick, long logs and rolled them close to the light of the
flames for us to use as benches.

Our first stop was the kitchen, though. The counselors might
not be the best cooks, but they did one thing right. Hot chocolate. It was a tradition. Every night at campfire time they set up
a couple of huge pots on a stove. Each pot is filled with hot
chocolate just barely cool enough to drink. I think it's their way
of apologizing for the other food they make us eat.

Just as we entered the kitchen cabin, Counselor Ted yelled
from the campfire. "Mike Andrews, use one of the mugs we left
beside the stove!"

Sure enough, Mike had brought along his special joke mug,
the one which takes up nearly a quarter of his knapsack. Not a
camping trip went by without Mike trying to pull one over on
the counselors by using his special mug. All Cadets are allowed
two helpings of hot chocolate for campfire sitting. I figured they

should let him drink two of his full mugs, just once. He'd be so sick he'd never look at hot chocolate again.

"Nuts," he said. When he picked up one of the normal mugs, a spider crawled out of it. "Great."

At the camp fire, all of the Cadets were quiet. The flames crackled up and down and the stars were so bright and clear against the darkness, all of us stared at the fire in a nice kind of silence.

Mr. Vanderhoek cleared his throat. "Sometimes God seems a little closer than at other times, doesn't He? Let's each offer a silent prayer of gratitude to Him for bringing us here safely, and for giving us this beauty among friends."

A few minutes later, murmured "Amens" were heard around the fire. In the quiet, Mr. Vanderhoek spoke again. "I want you to remember one thing, though, boys. God seems a little closer here only because it's so peaceful. Please don't forget that He's just as close when you're back in school or in a noisy place. You can pray to Him there too."

He started humming the tune to "Amazing Grace." He knew it was a favorite of ours on camping trips because it always sounded sweet in the silence of the woods, no matter how out of tune we were.

We sang the song, three verses worth, then broke into a faster-paced "Onward Christian Soldiers." By the time we finished that, we were in high spirits and ready to enjoy even the dumbest jokes a counselor might throw at us.

Mr. Vanderhoek started. "How come you can't starve in a desert?"

No answer.

"Because of all the sand which is there." He made it sound like "sandwiches there." We all groaned.

Counselor Ted said, "Why did the Cadet cross the road?" We all shouted back, "To get the chicken!" Then we hooted at

Counselor Ted. Every time we go camping, he forgets he's already told that one.

Suddenly three Cadets who had left for a bathroom break came crashing through the brush and stopped, gasping for breath, in front of the campfire. They trembled beside the counselors and looked behind them wildly.

"Haunted! Haunted! This place is haunted!" The first one could barely speak, he was so scared. "We saw an Indian ghost in war paint!" The other two shook their heads up and down in agreement; their faces were frozen white.

"OK," Mr. Vanderhoek said. "Speak slowly and tell us what happened."

I looked around for Joel. Mom would never forgive me if I let Joel get in trouble with Indian warriors. He was nowhere in sight, and I couldn't hear any bells.

"We were on our way back to our tent and we heard a rustling in the bushes. We thought it might be another Cadet trying to scare us, so we crept real close and shone our flashlights." He paused to catch his breath. "There he was!"

"What did it look like?"

"B-big!" He reached above his head to show how tall. "His hair was slicked straight back. There were dark streaks of war paint across his face and his skin was deathly white." All three shivered.

"Did he say anything?" Mr. Vanderhoek asked.

They shook their heads.

Mr. Vanderhoek thought for a few seconds. "One of you will have to lead Counselor Ted and me back to the spot where you saw this ghost. The rest of you stay here with the other counselors."

Counselor Ted asked, "Is everyone else here at the campfire?"

I said, "I don't see Joel. Of course, he may be close by."

Counselor Ted shouted, "Joel! Joel, get back to the camp-fire!"

I guess he still didn't know too much about Joel. I shouted, "Joel, I'm going to roast your teddy bear!" If he didn't come back to that, he wasn't ever coming back.

It was very quiet. I waited for a jangle of bells to let us know that Joel was nearby. A minute later it was still very quiet. I began to worry. Could there really be a ghost?

Worse, did it get my brother?

From behind us came a single crack. We all swung around and snapped on our flashlights. Above the edge of small bushes, there was the white face of an Indian ghost streaked with war paint!

"Aaaaagh!" Ralphy was the first one to shout.

The face disappeared. It had come and gone so quickly we didn't know whether to believe our eyes or not.

I was at the back edge of the Cadets who were now facing where we had last seen the warrior ghost. My voice was a whispery squeak. "Joooeeel. Get back here before your teddy gets crispy."

There was a tap on my shoulder, and I turned to see the warrior face! I jumped almost into the flames. "Aaaaaagh!" I reached for my jackknife.

Then I put it back into my pocket. I should have known who the warrior was.

"Here's your Indian warrior ghost, Cadets," Mr. Vanderhoek said. It was Joel. In the light of the flames, he still looked scary, even though he was much shorter than the warrior we had seen above the edge of the bushes. His hair was slicked back and there were streaks of mud over his face, his shirt, his arms, and his pants.

"Hello, Joel," Mr. Vanderhoek said. "Glad to see you made it back. Why do you have mud on your face?"

Joel shrugged shyly.

I finally dared try my voice. I looked at the bells and understood. "Umm, Mr. Vanderhoek? Ask Joel to shake his arms."

"Joel, please shake your arms," Mr. Vanderhoek said.

Joel shook his arms and grinned from behind the mud. There was no sound of jangling bells. Somewhere he had found mud and packed the bells with it to stop the jangling. Unfortunately, he had also plastered mud all over himself at the same time.

"But, Mr. Vanderhoek. The warrior we saw was a monster. At least ten feet tall!"

Mr. Vanderhoek walked around us and examined the area behind the edge of the bushes. He came back and gently took Joel's hand and led him to the spot. Mr. Vanderhoek motioned for the three Cadets to stand in front.

"Now shine your lights upward, all three of you." They did and we all took a half step backward. Joel was standing on a log behind the bushes. With the lights shining upwards and Joel blinking downwards, his face looked ghostly white and fierce behind the mud streaks. We all understood.

"Joel," Mr. Vanderhoek asked, "were you standing on a log in the woods too, the last time they shone light on you like this?"

Joel nodded. A sigh of relief circled the campfire like a gentle wind.

"Say good-night to your ghost, Cadets. I think it's time we all hit the sack."

No one grumbled at this one. It was time to relax.

Back in the tent, it took barely any time for us to be settled. All of us said our prayers and laid our heads back for sleep. All of us except for Mike. He propped himself on an elbow and stared out the open door of the tent.

"What's up, Mike?" I said. "There's no ghost out there."

"Just thinking." He grinned.

As I drifted off to sleep, I heard distant shouting and panic! It woke me quickly.

"What's that?" I hissed to Mike.

"New ghosts." He grinned again. "At the tent site Bruce and Jim took from us."

The shouting and panic became louder. When I looked out the tent to where Mike had been staring, I could see lights flashing and dark figures stumbling in the night.

"New g-ghosts?" Ralphy was sitting up and huddling his knees.

"Yup," Mike said. "New ghosts. Thousands of them no bigger than ants. In fact they *are* ants. Remember how carefully I swept that tent site?"

We nodded. Mike continued. "I figured Jim and Bruce would take it from us if they had a chance. There was a huge ant pile there, so I swept the top of it away. I guessed Jim and Bruce would be in such a hurry to take the tent site that they wouldn't look at the ground too close."

Mike giggled. "As Cadets of nature we all know most of the ants live underground, right? My only question was how long it would take for all those ants to get into their sleeping bags."

I snorted. In the faraway darkness, the shouting and panic only grew louder.

"Squirrrelll! Squirrrelll!"

We had just finished breakfast. That loud cry from nearby put everyone into action. The sound of running feet in the direction of the cry was like a stampede.

Unfortunately, it was my turn to do dishes, so I had to stay at the campsite. I knew what was happening, though.

Spot a squirrel and then yell. That's how to bring an avalanche of Cadets, all of them carrying sticks and pine cones. They circle the bottom of that tree and try to shake the squirrel loose. If that doesn't work, they throw pine cones—never rocks, which come down too hard—and sticks high into the branches to force the squirrel to hop into another tree.

Right after a squirrel chooses a new tree, the crowd scrambles over each other trying to make a new circle. And so on.

If the tree is too thick and the squirrel is too smart to be bothered by pine cones, a Cadet is sent up the tree. It used to be Ralphy's job because he is so small, but one time everybody forgot about him when the squirrel moved to a new tree, and he couldn't get down. By the time anyone remembered Ralphy, they forgot which tree he was in.

"Squirrreelllll! Squirrrrelllll!" By the sounds of it, the chase had already shifted three times.

Counselor Ted had stopped by to cook for us, which meant there were hunks of charred pancake to scrape before I could begin washing. The counselors rotate their cooking jobs from tent to tent so all the Cadets have a chance to suffer equally. They show us how to build proper cooking fires, and show us how to cook over a fire. With Counselor Ted, I knew we were in trouble as soon as he stirred the pancake batter with a branch. He called it getting back to the land. I called it a good way to add dirt and bugs to the batter when we had perfectly OK spoons.

"There he goes! No, the other tree!"

I wasn't missing much. No squirrel had ever been caught in our Cadet history. By now the squirrel had probably gone to its fourth or fifth tree. If it was a smart squirrel, it would jump into a bigger tree each time. Bigger trees are harder to shake.

There were only two toast-sized chunks of charcoal left in the pan when something tapped my arm. I nearly landed in the fire.

Sure enough, it was Joel.

I nearly yelled at him, but I saw his face. The mud was cleaned off, and I had removed his bells, but his features were crumpled with sadness.

"Was breakfast that bad?" I asked him.

He shook his head.

"Homesick?"

He shook his head again. Shouts interrupted me. "Squirrrreelllll! Next tree. We nearly got him now!"

Joel pointed in the direction of the shouts.

"Come here," I said. I checked carefully to make sure nobody was watching before I gave Joel a hug. It was a long hug.

"That old squirrel is twice as smart as any Cadet. He'll jump from tree to tree until he finds a way to disappear. It always works that way. In fact, sometimes I think squirrels don't bother hiding until they've had enough fun tiring out a bunch of stupid Cadets."

It worked. A little smile showed on Joel's face. Still, I decided I wouldn't chase squirrels next time the chance arrived. As usual, Joel was right—it wasn't fair. We found out later that others had noticed the same thing.

"Hi, guys," Mike said, stepping carefully over a pile of garbage I had stacked ready for disposal. I managed to give Joel a pat on the head before he disappeared.

"Don't hurt yourself avoiding the garbage you could throw away," I said.

"OK. Hey, Ricky, you better watch yourself today."

"What?"

He spoke louder. "You better watch yourself today."

"I heard you the first time. Just tell me what you meant."

He frowned a serious look of thought, the one that he fooled people with when he already knew what he was going to say. I sighed.

"Bruce and Jim are pretty mad at you."

"Bruce and Jim are mad at me?"

He nodded. "Yup. As a good friend I thought I should warn you. Nice guy, huh?"

"Mike, nice guys don't feed their best friend's comics to billy goats. Nice guys also don't take their friend's treasure map to the farm where they feed those billy goats. Let me guess. Somehow, Bruce and Jim think I'm the person who made them sleep on an ant pile last night."

Mike grinned. "Actually Randy Temples does. He had me pinned against a tree, so I had no choice but to confirm it for them."

"Mike, I never knew about the spot."

"You're so smart, I knew you'd have . . ."

"Asked someone to sweep it." I finished the sentence for him.

Mike continued. "Anyway, Randy's probably told Bruce and Jim. They already think you made Joel get them with the bramble bush trick. So I'd watch out."

"You're a wonderful friend."

"Poor guys," Mike said. "Bumps from ant bites everywhere. And no sleep either."

I giggled even though I was mad. Last night's shouting and panic had lasted for quite a while, even after the counselors had showed up with flashlights. Mike had a habit of making things interesting, even if it usually got me into trouble.

I had no choice but to be careful most of the day. Trying to convince Jim and Bruce that the ant pile was Mike's idea would make me look like a chicken. Probably nothing would have happened, either, except worrying about the outhouse made me forget Bruce and Jim later in the afternoon.

Outhouses are the worst things about camping trips. They are the dark clouds in your mind. No matter how much fun you're having, you know you will eventually have to face the outhouse. From day one of camp, its silhouette is a reminder that no Cadet can outwait it for the entire week.

The biggest spiders in the world build webs in outhouses because of the zillions of flies. You can check the inside carefully in the sunlight when the door is open, but you can't check underneath where you will be sitting. As soon as you close the door, it gets dark and you never know where the spiders might come from, and since they are so big you know they will be fast and mean.

Worse, nothing goes right or quickly when you need it most. Outhouses don't smell real good and they aren't built for comfort. Once you are actually inside with the door closed, you are in a hurry to finish, but that's not easy when you are sitting as lightly as possible to keep from getting slivers. Plus you are holding your breath.

Everyone reminds you it is a long ways down. Older Cadets always tell you about their cousin's friend's friend who fell through and had to wait for hours to be rescued.

The very worst part is noises. Who knows what can lurk underneath just waiting for an innocent Cadet to be in his most vulnerable position?

I knew if lunch was as bad as breakfast that the outhouse trip would have to be made much sooner than I wanted. That distraction is what led to trouble with Bruce and Jim.

Nothing unusual happened during the rest of the morning. Not even Ralphy's bumped head excited anyone.

"Warriors!" he shouted wildly, running into the middle of a knot-tying demonstration. Nobody looked up. We kept working on knots. Mike was sitting at the side of the group. His hands were tied together behind his back. Another string tied his hands to his neck.

What a dummy. Mike had actually believed I was going to show the rest of the Cadets a magic knot trick.

Ralphy held his head. He was used to bumps.

"That's nice," Counselor Ted said. "How many?"

"I don't know. I saw the face and started running!"

Mr. Vanderhoek said, "We'll look around after lunch." At every camp Ralphy heard noises nobody else heard.

"What's Mike doing?" Ralphy asked, glad to be able to change the subject after his report.

"It's a magic knot trick," I said. "If Mike gets out of those knots, we'll know he's magic."

Mike refused to speak. Counselor Ted thought it was funny seeing Mike finally get fooled, so he left him alone. I thought so too, especially with the dirty looks Jim and Bruce were glaring at me. We left Mike that way until lunch.

"I saw something, really," Ralphy said. "Right by the bend in the stream."

Later, when I was exploring the same part of the stream, I saw what could have been moccasin tracks, but Ralphy was always excited about something, so I didn't connect them to his story.

10

"Lunchtime is next, Fellows," Mr. Vanderhoek said. "Back to your campsites."

Mr. Vanderhoek turned to me. "Ricky, give us a head start before you undo those magic knots."

Great.

Mike was pretending to be friendly. That only meant he was ready to fight a bear as soon as the knots were untied. He hated being fooled. The good thing was it would only take a few minutes for him to see the funny side of it. Then he would be OK.

Everyone left.

"Magic knots, huh?"

"Mike, just a few simple knots. Not much for someone like you. I thought you'd be out of them in a jiffy."

"So maybe I was resting."

"You deserve to rest a lot longer after telling Jim and Bruce I planned the ant pile trick. Did you see the dirty looks they gave me?"

Mike bit off a giggle. "They want to tie you up pretty bad, I bet. Just get me out of these knots, and I'll think of a way to help you."

He didn't fool me for a second. All he wanted was to throw me in the lake. I went along with him.

"Turn around, Mike. I'll get these knots in a second."

"Hey! Not so rough, Pal."

I read somewhere how pickpockets work. If they want something from your back pocket, they bump your shoulder with one hand as they reach down with the other. The shoulder bump distracts you from feeling disturbance at your back pocket.

As I tugged hard at the knots with one hand, and leaned into Mike's shoulders, I worked on a little insurance with the other hand. After all the years with Mike, I knew better than to trick him without planning an escape route. He runs faster mad than I do scared. We both knew it.

"What kind of poison will we get for lunch?"

"Same old stuff," I said. If he wanted to pretend nothing would happen as soon as the knots were untied, so would I. "Just one more second, Mike. I've got half a knot to go."

He waited until he was sure both hands were free.

"Feel better?" I asked.

"Fine," he said. If I knew him, he would wait another five seconds, then draw a deep breath. The deep breath was like a bull pawing the ground. I edged backward slightly.

"Don't do it, Mike. We're even now after what you told Bruce and Jim."

"Magic knots!?!" He drew a deep breath.

I edged back a little more. "I think you should just call us even. It's for your own good, Mike."

"Start running, Pal, because you're going to be one sorry Cadet!" Mike never listens to good advice. He leaped forward. I put a good burst into my own running and hoped I had learned to tie a good knot.

Five steps. It was all he needed to get to full speed. Five steps. By then he was breathing down my neck.

Then, success, and I was safe as I heard a loud thump behind me. By the time I skidded to a stop, Mike was lying motionless on the ground. He only managed a halfhearted "ooooof" into the dirt in front of his face.

"I did warn you, Mike," I said.

"Ooooof."

Without turning over, Mike reached behind his back and felt the rope that was tied around his belt. When he decided to get up, he could follow the rope back to where it was tied around a small tree that was still shaking. I figured it was a good time to leave him alone.

* * * * * * * *

It was a quiet meal with Counselor Charlie. Mike was too stunned to talk. Joel was too hungry to talk. Ralphy and me were too worried about Counselor Charlie's cooking to talk.

"Great meal, Boys. Just smell this outdoor cooking." Counselor Charlie whistled as he mixed a stew together. "Yup, this'll put hair on your chest. Nothing like the great outdoors to make a man feel alive. Little bit of this chow and you'll be roaring for days, yup."

Counselor Charlie never needed answers to keep talking. He was happy to squat in front of the fire, humming and mixing food in the pot with the spoon he had tied onto the end of a long branch.

"Pretty smart, huh, Guys. This is one counselor who doesn't like burning himself. Put a spoon on the end and stir from a distance, I always say. Necessity is the mother of invention. Camping is the life, yup."

He started slopping stew into our bowls.

After one or two tastes, we felt like slopping it onto the

ground. I was lucky. Joel looked at me with bright eyes and an empty bowl. I gave him the rest of my stew. Ralphy and Mike had to find excuses to walk into the trees and accidently spill their bowls. Even Counselor Charlie had a tough time finishing his meal.

"Well, Boys," he coughed. "Good, huh? Who's doing dishes?"

It was Mike's turn. Counselor Charlie left early, probably to search for better food at another tent, so Mike got lazy about it.

He gathered the dishes together and pointed at the nearby stream. "That tap is plenty big enough for a few small dishes."

"Are you sure that's OK?" Ralphy asked. "We're supposed to use the bucket and empty it into a garbage pit."

"The sooner you fill a garbage pit, the sooner you have to dig another one," Mike said.

Later, I wished I would have stopped Mike from dumping the leftover stew into the stream. But I was too worried about an ordeal ahead of me to say anything.

My immediate problem was dealing with my worst fear, the outhouse. I decided to get it over with. Otherwise I would spend the entire afternoon worrying.

It took too short a time getting there, even though I trudged as slowly as I could, and stopped as often as possible to examine bugs on the ground or birds in the sky. It was a nice day, and walking through the trees and grass under such a blue sky should have made me whistle. Instead, I gulped.

The door creaked open. I held it wide, trying to get as much sunlight in there as I could. It didn't look bad. I took a deep breath and swung the door shut. There was only a little hole cut through the wood for a window. I waited for half a minute, listening for any unusual noises in the near darkness. Nothing.

By then I was running out of air. I needed to take another breath, so I took a gasp as quickly as possible. My heart pounded.

I gave it some thought, and decided I really could wait another day without hurting myself. I darted outside into the fresh air and nearly bumped into Counselor Ted.

"How's Joel doing?" he asked.

"Fine," I said. "He's . . ." *Where was Joel?* ". . . probably at the tent waiting for me. I'm just going there now."

As I left, I heard Counselor Ted creak open the outhouse door.

I didn't find Joel back at the tent. Ralphy was there trying to read my comic books.

He looked up. "What'd you do to these? Every time I get to a good part, the ink is a mess like you left it in the rain and ran over it with your bicycle."

"It's a long story, Ralphy. Have you seen Joel?"

"He followed you when you left here."

Great.

He had his teddy bear, so I had no way of forcing him into the open. With luck, he would still be near the outhouse, looking for the five-foot-high toads I had warned him about. Most kids would get scared. Joel wanted one or two to replace his garter snake collection.

Since I was trying to sneak up on him, I went quietly. From a distance, I saw him behind a tree doing his favorite thing—being invisible and watching other people.

In front of the outhouse, Jim and Bruce were struggling to carry a huge bucket. From the water slooshing over top, it looked full of dirty dishwater.

It was nearly quiet in the heat of the afternoon. There was the shouting of Cadets, of course. That never stopped. Neither did the echoing clop of axes and hatchets against wood. It seemed everyone had their favorite tree to bring down by the end of the week. Cadets usually went back to it whenever they had the energy, and chopped until they were tired or remembered something better to do.

Since I had to be quiet enough to sneak up on the world's best sneaker, Jim and Bruce had no idea I was nearby. Neither did Joel.

As I watched, Jim and Bruce lifted the bucket together and gave it a mighty upwards shove. Gallons of dirty, soapy water shot through the outhouse window halfway up the wall.

Both started cackling and howling.

Jim shouted, "Hey, Ricky, how does that feel? As good as ant bites?"

Bruce was rolling on the ground and gasped, "Or does it feel as good as bramble bushes?"

They howled louder and clapped each other on the back.

"Need a bath, Ricky? Hah, hah, hah."

Joel had his hand over his mouth. He was hopping up and down in excitement as he watched. It was easy to step right behind him and watch over his shoulder.

I suddenly realized Jim and Bruce must have followed me to the outhouse, raced back for the water, and missed seeing me leave early!

The outhouse door creaked open. Counselor Ted stepped into the sunlight. His belt was still undone. From his head down to his toes, he was sopping wet. His hair hung down and dripped water onto his nose. He blew hard with his mouth and sprayed water into the air.

Jim and Bruce choked in mid-howl.

Counselor Ted stepped forward. His shoes squeaked in the sudden silence. In front of me, a snicker slipped out from Joel's hand. He still didn't know I was behind him.

Counselor Ted stared long and hard at Jim and Bruce. Their mouths were frozen open in horror.

Counselor Ted finally spoke. "My name isn't Ricky," he said solemnly.

Joel snickered again and turned to leave. He bumped into me. "Aaaak!" When he landed, his face was white. Camps sure are fun.

11

"Mike, you carry the frying pan. It's getting heavy."

We were a half mile upstream from camp. It was Tuesday afternoon, and time was going much too quickly.

Earlier, Mike had decided to find some gold nuggets in the stream, but wouldn't admit he was too nervous to go alone. I agreed to go only after he called a truce, just in case he had ideas about getting me back for the magic knot trick.

He took the pan as we walked. It was heavy, but Mike said it would be worthwhile when we panned nuggets from the gravel.

After turning two more corners of the stream, I said, "Mike, we gotta go back."

"Tell me again the look on Counselor Ted's face." Mike was upset he had missed the outhouse action.

"I already have, only about a hundred times since we started trailblazing. Now I'm telling you we gotta go back."

"I wonder how many potatoes they'll have to peel."

"Mike, you heard me."

He groaned. "You want to go back because you're still worried about that hatchet?"

"No, it's not because my hatchet is gone." Mike just wouldn't understand why I was upset about losing it. "You don't know how important a hatchet is, do you? If you ever read, you would know a hatchet is the most important tool for surviving in the bush. If you have only a hatchet and matches, you can almost live forever in the bush. *If* you know what to do. That's why I always carry a survival kit."

I patted the small box I had strapped to my belt. "Of course, fishing line helps too, if you want to rough it. You can catch fish and snare rabbits and—"

"I know, Ricky, I know. You tell me so many times, I think maybe you want to get lost in the woods someday. How about telling me why we should go back after getting this far. Gold nuggets are worth a fortune these days."

"Joel."

"Joel? He's not following us. He's stuck on the chocolate bar trick."

As far as I knew, Joel was occupied with emergency preparation number two. I tie four chocolate bars on a string and hang them from a branch just out of his reach. Through experimenting, I know what height is far enough to be unreachable but close enough to keep him trying.

Hung perfectly, the bars get twenty or thirty jumps out of Joel before he decides to leave and find out what I'm doing. It is only a temporary surrender. Before he gets within sneaking distance of me, he remembers the chocolate bars, but forgets he can't reach them. Joel is a true optimist. He then drops the chase and heads back to the chocolate bars. The coming and going keeps him out of my hair for as long as two hours.

"Mike, I think I'm going crazy. I get mad when Joel follows me, but I worry about leaving him alone. What should I do?"

"We'll go back." Mike is a true friend. "Besides, I'm pretty tired of marking these trees," he said.

I sighed. Mike just couldn't get the hang of surviving in the woods. If only he read more books instead of feeding them to billy goats.

"You gotta mark trees, Mike. How else can you find your way around strange areas?"

"Easy. Follow this stream we keep stepping in. I'll bet Davy Crockett didn't mark trees with a perfectly good stream nearby," Mike said.

"I'll bet he did, just to practice for when he needed it. What happens when we leave the stream?"

"Our feet get dry again."

"And we'll be pretty good at trailblazing too, won't we."

It was easy walking most of the time. There were gravel beds along the stream. Once in a while, the water got deep and then we would have to climb the bank and walk through the thick bushes.

"Ricky, do you believe in ghosts?" Mike was serious for a change.

"That old guy at the grocery store was just trying to scare us with the story about Indian legends," I said. "Right?"

"I knew that. Silly question." He paused. "But in general, do you think there could be such things as ghosts?"

"There sure are a lot of stories, aren't there? Like haunted houses and things like that. It makes you wonder. Especially at night in the woods," I said. "And don't talk about it in the tent. Ralphy has enough trouble falling asleep."

Mike nodded. I said, "We'll ask Mr. Vanderhoek tonight at the fire. He usually has good answers to tough questions."

Mike stopped me by grabbing my arm. He pointed wordlessly ahead. A broken branch was pinned into one of our trailblazing marks. The branch was long and skinny. It was painted in grays and reds and blacks. Tied on the middle and hanging downwards were two long dark feathers, ruffling gently in the breeze.

Pinned by the branch into the tree was a Cadet shirt. I nearly jumped into Mike's arms. It was slashed in dozens of places. Where the badges had been ripped from the material, a dark, dark stain was spreading!

"Ricky, that's not. . ."

"It can't be," I whispered.

A thick red liquid dripped from the shirt. Already flies buzzed frantically as they fought to land in the center of the stain.

Mike and I looked around very carefully and tiptoed backward.

"Don't even say it, Ricky."

I said it as fast as I could. "That's-blood-a-whole-bunch-of-blood-and-it's-still-fresh-and-we-should-be-running-as-fast-as-we-can-instead-of-standing-here-holding-a-stupid-frying-pan."

I had wasted my breath on him. Mike was ten yards away and crashing through branches as he gained speed, even with the frying pan clutched tightly in his hand.

I chased him all the way to camp. We had never run faster.

Most everybody was down at the lake. Either they were taking canoe lessons or watching the others take canoe lessons. Mr. Vanderhoek stood by the edge, shouting encouragement across the water.

We nearly ran him over. Then we had to stop and breathe. Mr. Vanderhoek waited patiently.

Finally, Mike gasped. "Get all the Cadets together! We gotta find out who's missing!"

A good thing about counselors is that they don't panic easy. Mr. Vanderhoek's half-smile at our exhaustion became a look of concern, but he only drew us aside.

"Get your breath. Speak quietly so the others don't get upset. Tell me what is wrong."

Mike explained. As he spoke, I pictured the shirt. Something about it tugged at the back of my mind.

"OK," he said quietly. "Go wait for me by the edge of camp. I'll get the counselors to gather everyone for a head count. Then I'll meet you there."

"And Mike, if this is one of your jokes—" He stopped himself. I think he knew we were biting our lips not to show fear, or tears.

"That's okay, Guys. We'll get to the bottom of this."

As we walked away, he shouted to the rest. "Tent inspection in five minutes! Messiest campers peel potatoes for tonight's feast!" I was too upset to point out that rock-hard potatoes with peelings on them aren't much of a feast.

Mr. Vanderhoek took a few minutes privately explaining to the counselors that they needed to make sure everyone was still at camp. When he finished, and as he strode toward us, something hit me.

Joel! In our panic to get back, I had forgotten about Joel.

Mr. Vanderhoek noticed. "Ricky, what's the matter?"

"Joel . . ."

He understood immediately. "Mike," he said, "can you lead me back to the tree?"

"All we need to do is follow the trailblazing marks."

"OK. Ricky, look for Joel, but be careful. Remember two things. Joel usually disappears, but he takes care of himself. And trust God."

I nodded. They left and I sprinted to the chocolate bar tree. It was about fifty yards past our tent. As I got closer, I slowed down, looking for a slight movement that might betray Joel's spying position.

There was no use yelling for him because he associated my yelling with bad news. Which was usually the case. I could see the strings hanging from the tree. Five steps closer and I saw something which chilled me. No chocolate bars!

Without the chocolate bars, Joel could be anywhere. I didn't have his teddy bear as insurance.

"Joel," I said low and urgent. "Jooooeeel!"

Nothing. Not even a flicker of movement to show where he was watching me from. I didn't like being so desperate to find him that I had to stoop to nasty tricks. I did anyway.

"Joel, I've got a squirrel here with a broken leg. It's crying little squirrel tears and it needs your help." I would try explaining later to Joel why I lied.

Not even that popped him into the open. There was only the breeze pushing against the tops of trees and the cawing of far away crows. I felt like crying. Where was he?

I walked in big circles, explaining in a loud voice how badly a poor squirrel needed Joel's help. When he didn't pop out of nowhere to scare me into my usual heart attack, I knew he wasn't in the area.

I went back to the middle of the camp, where we had our nightly bonfires. The counselors and the rest of the Cadets were there, all waiting for Mike and Mr. Vanderhoek to return. There was nothing else I could do.

* * * * * * * *

Mr. Vanderhoek motioned for me to join him just out of earshot from the rest of the Cadets.

"No sign of Joel?" Mr. Vanderhoek's lips were tight with grimness.

I shook my head.

"The shirt was gone," Mike said. "But we found blood on the ground and a hole punched into the tree where the branch had stuck the shirt. It's enough to make you believe in Indian spirits."

"Mike, that kind of talk only makes everyone upset," Mr. Vanderhoek said gently.

"Sorry," Mike said. He too could tell I was upset. "Ricky,

don't worry. Remember? That was a Cadet shirt on the tree. Joel's too young to own one."

Suddenly I knew what was bothering me about the shirt. Joel liked wearing my Cadet stuff because it made him feel special. That's why he had taken my hat from the buried treasure back in Jamesville.

Once he had tried writing his name on the collar of the Cadet shirt with Mom's lipstick. Naturally, he did it five minutes before a Cadet parade in church. Not all of the lipstick came off, but Mom told me it was a badge of honor because my younger brother was trying so hard to be like me.

My face must have turned white.

"Ricky, what is it?"

"That was my shirt on the tree. We ran away so fast, it didn't hit me. But that was my shirt." Thinking back to the shirt stuck into the tree, I pictured the blotch on the collar.

"The collar had an old mark on it that I recognized. And Joel wore it as often as he could sneak it away from me."

Mr. Vanderhoek turned immediately and stepped onto a log to address the group. "Listen up. Everyone back to their tents. Your counselors will join you shortly to give further instructions. Ricky's brother Joel is missing and you will begin a search in five minutes."

He paused, wondering if he should tell more. "One other thing. Did somebody play a terrible joke with a Cadet shirt? Please tell me now if you did."

Nobody stirred. "OK. Anybody sees a shirt where it shouldn't be, tell your counselor immediately. Any questions?"

Ralphy stuck his hand into the air. "I just saw a shirt. It was hanging on the outhouse door but I didn't go close because . . ."

Ralphy hated outhouses.

"I'll check that out," Mr. Vanderhoek said. "Everyone to their tent sites."

Mr. Vanderhoek gave the counselors their instructions for where to search, then took Mike, Ralphy, and me toward the outhouse. As we got closer, it was obvious that it was my shirt hanging on the outside door handle. The blood had dried to a brown-red.

Suddenly, there was a creaking from inside!

Ralphy, Mike, and I jumped. Mr. Vanderhoek moved us behind him. We approached carefully. The creaking grew a little louder. We stopped about five feet from the door.

It began to open slowly! Into the sunlight stepped—Joel. In one hand he carried the red, gray, and black painted stick.

I nearly fainted. Joel closed the door very carefully and smiled shyly. He squinted upwards but didn't look surprised to see us. "All done," he said. "Someone next?"

He grabbed the shirt from the door handle. "Very dirty, Ricky. But I keep it a secret for you. Won't tell Mom, I promise."

I didn't know whether to hug or kill him.

Mr. Vanderhoek said, "You can put the frying pan down now, Mike."

Behind me, frozen in shock, Mike still held the frying pan high above his head, ready to bash any Indian spirits who came near.

"Did you guys see any potatoes?" Counselor Ted asked as he walked up to our tent. We had a little fire crackling as the afternoon light was fading away. Joel was sitting nearby, relaxing in the warmth.

To him, there was nothing strange about the afternoon's events. "Chocolate bars gone. Follow you. Find your shirt in tree," he said every time I asked him.

Nothing I did could convince him to say anything more. Which wasn't unusual.

I would just have to be happy with the fact that he was nearby to smile at my foolish persistence in asking questions.

Would a Cadet steal the four chocolate bars? I hoped not. But thinking of ghosts, I almost hoped so.

Counselor Ted sat down beside us.

"Potatoes?" Mike said. "Mr. Vanderhoek was serious about having potatoes tonight? Didn't we go through enough today?"

"Yup. Bruce and Jim peeled five pots full, but all the pots disappeared while we were looking for Joel."

"We wouldn't have been able to eat them anyway," Mike said.

"Why not?" Counselor Ted asked.

"Because Ricky lost his hatchet, and we have nothing else big enough to mash them. The four of us here wouldn't have been able to eat them without it."

Counselors had a habit of turning potatoes into rocks you could barely split with a knife. The odd time the potatoes came out soft, they were pieces of mush that fell through your fork.

"Very funny," Counselor Ted said. A strange look crossed his face. "Your hatchet, too? My ax is gone. About a dozen others have asked me the same question tonight."

"How do you like that," I said. "All of our most important survival tools gone. Did you know that if you only have a hatchet and matches, you can almost live forever in the bush? If you know what to do. Of course, fishing line helps too. With fishing line, you can catch fish and snare rabbits and stitch cuts —"

"If the potatoes are gone, what's for supper?" Mike asked.

"Hot dogs."

We cheered. Even counselors couldn't ruin hot dogs. I forgave Mike for interrupting me.

Half an hour later, we had nothing to cheer about. I was wrong about counselors and hot dogs. One of them had packed the ice on top of the hot dog buns in the food coolers. Ice blocks had first crushed the buns, then broke holes in the plastic and soaked them with water.

Right after you pull it back from the flames, roasted to perfection, there is no way to hold a hot dog without using a bun. The hot dog is too hot. Even if you wait for it to cool down, you need to use something to hold the relish and ketchup and mustard. In other words, we had no choice but to wrap delicious juicy hot dogs with soggy lumps of dough. Joel ate five.

"Guys," I said, "in two minutes we'll be going to the big campfire for hot chocolate. As a favor to me, can you avoid drinking it by the gallon?"

"Why?" Ralphy asked.

Mike grinned. "I know why. Ricky's tired of being stepped on every time you guys have to leave the tent at night. You go running out, then run back in twice as fast."

"I heard something move last night," Ralphy said. "You'd run too."

"Sure, Ralphy," Mike said, choosing not to remember his own dash of panic with me. Already Ralphy's flashlight batteries were dead. He was always the first Cadet to use up all his light. Sometimes he would keep the flashlight on in his sleeping bag to fall asleep.

After supper, since his flashlight was dead, Ralphy walked between me and Mike as we went to the campfire.

Joel was somewhere nearby. We couldn't hear him, of course. I had his teddy bear, though. For the rest of camp, my goal was to keep him safe.

At the fire, it was a little quieter than usual.

"Was it really blood on your shirt?" Harvey Voortel asked. He was one of the biggest Cadets, so if he was nervous, everyone else was for sure.

"I think so," I said. "At least Mike ran away fast enough."

Mike said, "And who was right behind me?"

"Only because I know you're afraid to be alone in the woods."

Mr. Vanderhoek quieted everyone by raising his hands. "We've been blessed with another day in the woods, and we're here together to enjoy the evening. Let's take a moment to silently thank our Lord."

In the quiet, the fire cracked and popped and insects made their *creak-creak* noises in the bushes behind us. In my prayer, I thanked God that Joel was still around to scare me whenever I wasn't ready for his appearances.

"Time for counselor talk," Mr. Vanderhoek said. "We're starting to get lazy on important things here in the woods.

"First of all, don't do your dishes in the lake or the stream. Sure, it only seems like a little soap, but that's not the point. Your reverence for God should include reverence for His creation.

"Second, little campfires only at your tents. And don't leave them unattended. Big fires waste wood. Big campfires also lead to big forest fires if you don't watch them.

"Third," Mr. Vanderhoek grinned. "If you are going to help someone wash up, ask them for permission beforehand. Bruce and Jim will be peeling potatoes for the next three nights because they thought Counselor Ted was too dirty!"

The hooting and hollering around the campfire broke up the serious mood. Even Jim and Bruce had to laugh.

"To make up for last night's joke, Ralphy has a poem," Counselor Ted said. "Everybody knows how he likes to make them."

Ralphy shyly stood and read it to us. I shone a flashlight over his shoulder. It was even funnier to read it from the paper:

Oh would that I wuz a riemer
With ritten werd in tenths and timer.

Cuz if eye beed a noted poet
Persuns would bee interested in things I sayed and roet.

Maebe sum dae famus I'd becum
Writing vers and never scum

Making young minds both kwik and inspired
Reeding my stuff befour they retired.

Ralphy was so relieved that we liked his poem, he promised to make another one for the next campfire.

I didn't have a poem or a joke, but I raised my hand anyway.

"Mr. Vanderhoek, do you believe in ghosts?"

Around the campfire, it got quiet again. Mr. Vanderhoek thought a while before answering.

"No, Ricky, I don't believe in ghosts. I don't think any Christian does."

"But what about all the stories you hear? Haunted houses. Things that can't be explained. Maybe even the ripped shirt today."

I continued. "I mean, where do legends and stories get started? Isn't there a saying 'where there's smoke, there's fire'?"

Mr. Vanderhoek nodded. "Yes, and the saying means behind every story there is usually some truth. But I said, 'Christians don't believe *in* ghosts.' Christians believe *in* Jesus."

He smiled. "I'm not playing word games. It's important to know in whom you really believe before talking about ghosts and spirits and such things. If you asked me if I believed there were ghosts, I would have to say I don't have the answer."

Mike interrupted. "You mean there really are ghosts?!?"

"Mike," Mr. Vanderhoek said, "I don't know enough to give you a 'yes' or a 'no.' But I don't believe in ghosts the way you usually think of ghosts. If you think that ghosts are the spirits of people who have died, no, I don't believe in them. But . . . there are . . . some things . . . that just can't be explained. We don't know for sure."

Everyone at the campfire leaned closer to listen. Mr. Vanderhoek thinks his answers through before giving them and he always looks at things from both sides.

"If you know history," he continued, "you know about Benjamin Franklin and his kite. They say he discovered electricity, but really, he didn't. It was there all the time. For example, hundreds of years ago, when only Indians lived by this lake, electricity was here. They didn't know what it was because it was outside of their knowledge and their senses."

"But they could see lightning," Mike said.

"How could they know it was electricity? Except for lightning, you can't see electricity. You can't hear it. If you are ever unlucky enough to get a tiny shock, it feels like an angry bite. If you had never heard of electricity or seen it used, you wouldn't know about it. All agreed?"

We nodded.

"What I am trying to tell you is this. Benjamin Franklin discovered something that was there all the time—electricity—and today all of us take it for granted. By so doing, he showed that we as humans in God's world don't know everything."

I like it when Mr. Vanderhoek talks to us like we're big enough to sometimes think seriously about things. He knows we're not just a bunch of kids. It was quiet around the campfire.

"It would be silly to believe that we know everything now," he said quietly. "Just because something is unseen and undiscovered, it doesn't mean we can say it doesn't exist."

"Awesome idea," Mike said.

Mr. Vanderhoek grinned. "Perfect timing, Mike. I was just going to talk about the word *reverence*. It means 'respectful awe,' and when we older folks start preaching, we use the word too often and too easily. We wear it out."

Mr. Vanderhoek seemed to forget about us as he talked. His eyes stared far away into the fire.

"To have respectful awe takes some fear. I think we sometimes lose that fear when we talk about God. Yes, He loves us, but He is as big as forever and mightier than the worst storms and earthquakes we can imagine. By thinking we know everything, we lose that fear, that respectful awe. . ."

He snapped out of it and smiled. "So, Ricky, I cannot say for sure there are ghosts or there are no ghosts. It is beyond what we can know. But believe this, a world with or without ghosts is still God's world. Miracles happen. If you permit mystery in your world, you'll have more fun in life. And you won't take God for granted."

I have to admit, as I walked back to the tent after the campfire, it felt good to be in a world with a lot of things to discover and wonder about.

I crawled into my sleeping bag, enjoying my thoughts, and I nearly yelped. Something cold touched my leg!

I recovered enough to shine my flashlight down my sleeping bag. It was my hatchet. I didn't say a word. If someone was playing a practical joke, they weren't about to get the satisfaction of hearing my surprise. Then I shivered. On the edges of the steel, I noticed slight traces of red and black and gray paint.

"Yeeaaaaghhhh!"

A fiercely painted Indian was swooping down on me as I frantically fought the thick bushes which kept me from running!

"Yeeaaaaggghhhh!"

I kicked and kicked, but nothing could free my legs. It was as if I was wrapped tightly in a sleeping bag. Just before the war hatchet came crashing down on me, I woke up. My sleeping bag was twisted underneath me and I could barely move.

Great.

It was Wednesday morning. I didn't want time to be passing so quickly. So much to do with only a few days left.

I opened my eyes. Almost right above me, Ralphy was staring down at my face.

"Yeeaaaaggghhhh!" He screamed in fright. I nearly popped through the roof of the tent.

"Ralphy," I said, " 'Good morning' is usually a nicer way to wake someone up."

He put his hand over his mouth and pointed at my face.

"Mmmmpphhhh."

I shook my head. "You've finally flipped, Ralphy. Or did a counselor force you to eat breakfast?"

He backed out of the tent, still staring at me with his eyes bugging out of his face.

I yawned and stretched. It had been a weird night of sleep. First, there was my hatchet. Finding it in my sleeping bag was crazy enough. Falling asleep the night before, I had told myself the flecks of paint were probably my imagination. No use making everyone else worry. I would check it out in the sunlight.

Second, I had dreamed about Indian spirits all night. That didn't surprise me after what had happened with the shirt, but the dreams seemed so real. It felt like I had tossed and turned and seen Indian spirits every time I opened my eyes.

Third, there was the way Ralphy woke me up, screaming at me like that. I thought during camp the only alarm clock would be birds chirping nicely at dawn.

It takes a lot of patience to begin a day when you're camping. Summer nights can sometimes still be cold. If you actually get out of your sleeping bag to dress, you nearly break your teeth chattering in the cold. Nothing makes you hop more than putting on icy blue jeans, so you have to go gradually.

I grabbed my clothes from where I was lying and stuffed them into my sleeping bag. After a few minutes, they were warm enough to wear. I began the tricky part of dressing inside the sleeping bag with only my face sticking out into the cold air.

Joel popped his head inside the tent.

"Aaak," he said after a quick look at me, and left.

What did he know about dressing, anyway. Dressing in a sleeping bag was normal for smart campers. Just before stepping outside, I remembered my hatchet.

I grabbed it and fumbled through the tent flaps. The sky was bright blue already, and even though the air was still cool, the sun was shining bright. It was going to be a good day.

I stretched and yawned, reaching for the sky. The weight of the hatchet in my hand felt good. I pushed the stretch as hard as I could.

"Hey, Ricky," Mike said from behind me. "You should have seen Ralphy and Joel take off from here. It was like they saw a ghost."

I turned around, still stretching, with my hatchet held high.

"Yipes!" Mike jumped two feet straight up.

I sure had strange tentmates. "Give me a break, Mike. I'm just stretching." I set the hatchet down.

He peered at me. "Oh, that is you." Then he started laughing crazily. Pretty soon he was rolling on the ground.

"What's so funny?" I said. He wouldn't answer.

Fine. I examined my hatchet in the sunlight. Sure enough, there were little flecks of paint on the steel. Gray and red and black. Mr. Vanderhoek would need to see this.

"Mike, I'm going to find a counselor."

That made him laugh harder. Maybe the sun was shining, but it looked like it was going to be a weird day. I left him there on the ground near the tent.

I walked towards the counselors' cabin, holding my hatchet carefully close to me to keep any bushes from rubbing the paint flecks from it. There seemed to be little activity around the campground.

The mistake I made was to worry about spider webs. When I got to the counselors' cabin, there were spider webs with little drops of dew all across the front of the door. Instead of reaching through the webs with my hand to knock, I pounded on the door with the back end of my hatchet.

No answer. I pounded again and the door opened, halfway through one of my swings.

It was Counselor Ted, hair sticking straight up and looking groggy in only a T-shirt and shorts. He blinked once and screamed. I jumped, still holding my hatchet high. He screamed again.

"I'll save us," he shouted.

I looked behind me to see what was coming. Suddenly, it felt like ten bears had landed on top of me.

"Come here! Come here!" Counselor Ted screamed. "I got him! I got him!"

Whatever it was, I hoped Counselor Ted would get it off me quickly. My face was smushed right into the ground, and I could barely breathe.

"Let him go." It was Mr. Vanderhoek.

"But he'll get away."

"I hope so," Mr. Vanderhoek said. "Whatever it is you think you have, it's wearing running shoes. I think that makes it a Cadet."

Hold it. I was wearing running shoes.

The weight on top of me disappeared and I rolled over to see all the counselors staring down on top of me. None of them were dressed.

Counselor Ted brushed pine needles and dirt off his T-shirt. "It is a Cadet," he said accusingly. "Next time you play a prank like that, especially with a hatchet in your hand, you might not be so lucky." He looked at the other counselors. "I say he peels potatoes."

"I was knocking on the door," I said. "I wanted to show you something about my hatchet."

"At six in the morning?"

"The birds are up," I pointed out. I picked my hatchet from the dirt. "I was going to show you paint on my hatchet. I found it in my sleeping bag last night, after it was gone all day, and it had small bits of gray and red and black paint on it, just like on the branch we saw yesterday."

My hatchet was too dirty to show anything. The counselors

were still staring at me strangely.

"I'm sorry for waking you," I said. "It's just that this seemed important after what has been happening."

Nobody broke the silence. It looked like I would be peeling potatoes for sure. They kept staring.

Finally, Mr. Vanderhoek spoke. "All that is fine, Ricky. But why do that to your face? After what's been happening, I don't think it is too appropriate. Especially with younger Cadets who can be scared so easily."

"What?" I said.

Mr. Vanderhoek walked to the tree that had his shaving basin hanging from a branch. He grabbed his mirror and brought it over to me.

"It's a mean thing to do, Ricky." He held the mirror in front of me.

Not one inch looked like my face. Dark paint covered my chin, my cheeks and my forehead. Savage white and red streaks started on my nose and fanned across my cheeks. I grinned weakly at the counselors. Then I fainted.

* * * * * * * *

"Cute, Kid, very cute."

I was in bare feet and wearing only my blue jeans as I tiptoed down to the edge of the lake on tender feet. My face needed washing.

"Who's that!" I quickly draped my towel over my bare chest. The voice had sounded distinctly female.

Sheila, the girl from the general store, stepped out from behind a tree ahead of me.

"Call me the milkman," she said. "I'm the person who brings fresh supplies to camp."

I pulled the towel tighter. "Milkmen don't spy," I said. "Besides, you're not old enough to drive a truck."

"Down back roads I am. It's not that far to the store, and my dad says I can do anything that any boy can." Her eyes flashed and reminded me of Lisa Higgins. Her next statement proved me right.

"And if you're too much of a city slicker to hear me coming up the path, then you deserve to be spied on."

"Fine," I said. "Just fine." Somehow, I had a feeling she had not been walking up the path, but that she had been hiding for some time. At that moment, however, I was too embarrassed at my condition to make it an issue.

"Nice makeup," she said. "Is this something all of you in this group do?"

Why was she so determined to be nasty?

"As a matter of fact, only the bravest of us are allowed the honor," I said. "And I am modestly about to wash it away because I don't like showing off."

She laughed. "Right. Or maybe some spirits did it."

What did she know?

Unfortunately, I didn't have time to ask. My next step landed my right foot on a huge thistle and I howled and landed on a slippery rock and fell into the lake.

When I surfaced, she was gone.

Looking stupid like that was the main reason I didn't mention her to anyone when I got back to the tent site.

"Washed your blue jeans along with your face, Ricky?"

"A wise man would ask no questions right now, Mike," I said.

"A wise man wouldn't put makeup on his face in the first place."

"Mike, I don't even want to think about it."

"But how could you not know what was happening?"

"Maybe because I was fast asleep and thought I was dreaming about Indian spirits. It could just as easily happen to you if you had the front of the tent."

"No way," he said. "I'd wake up and catch anybody who was painting my face. Then they'd pay."

"Right." It chilled me to think about somebody—or worse, something—carefully painting my face and then vanishing.

I looked around and shivered. The woods seemed to press in darkly. I wanted nothing more than to be in Jamesville. Camping wasn't fun at all, at least not camping with Indian spirits.

Mr. Vanderhoek was cooking at our tent site.

Ralphy hauled his knapsack out of the tent to get his dishes. "Boy, I'm hungry." he said. He reached into his knapsack, then yelped and dropped it. "Something's alive in there!"

It got Joel's attention. He strolled over and peered inside. He stuck his hand deep into the knapsack. A mouse shot up his arm, over his shoulder and hit the ground running. Joel giggled. Ralphy sighed with relief.

Ralphy pulled out his plate, then moaned. "I hate mice," he said. Arranged in a neat line across the middle were little brown pellets. When he shook his plate at arm's length, only one pellet dropped.

"Can I use your plate when you're finished, Ricky?" he asked.

I laughed until I cried, and when I finished laughing, the woods seemed brighter and camping was fun again. Spirits or no spirits.

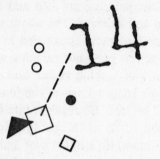

14

"I'm going to the lake before our hike," Mike said. "Ralphy's taking canoe lessons."

The counselors taught us in groups because there weren't enough canoes for all the Cadets. Mike expected Ralphy would find a way to sink all the canoes on the lake at once.

Later, after lunch, all of us Cadets were going on a hike. That would take most of Wednesday afternoon.

"Count me out," I said. "I'm going to try spying on Joel. I think he knows more than he lets on about these strange happenings."

I decided not to mention running into Sheila, even though she could be described as a stranger. Perhaps I should have. Instead, I continued, "I wish Joel would talk more. He sees and notices things that normal people wouldn't discover in a hundred years of looking. And you know what?"

Mike shook his head.

"If there really were spirits, Joel wouldn't be afraid. He'd walk right up to them and pretend they were as common as the wild squirrels he manages to feed."

"Now, that's a scary thought."

There was a movement in the bushes to my right. No noise, of course. Joel doesn't make noise when he moves. He was heading on his mysterious routes through the woods.

"Did you forget the extra bread for feeding squirrels?" I shouted in the direction of the movement.

Joel would pause to think about it. Extra bread was news to him, since I had just thought it up. He would carefully circle the camp, and watch for anything unusual before stepping back to the campfire area. That gave me a few minutes to get the bread.

"Mike, I gotta run. Don't throw anything at Ralphy as he canoes," I joked. "And please don't tell him about any man-eating fish in the lake."

He grinned. I darted into our tent to dig deep into my knap-sack. At the bottom, I found my last sandwhich. Three days old and very stale, it was still worth considering. For a moment, I was tempted to eat it in two gulps instead of setting it on the ground beside the firepit for Joel to take.

When I stepped out again, Mike was gone. Of course, there was no sign of Joel.

"Wait for me," I shouted in the direction of the lake. I ran after Mike, then stopped and circled back to camp. Joel wasn't the only one with a few tricks.

By the way he looked at the sandwich, I could tell he was tempted to eat it too. Just then, the whirring of squirrel chatter distracted him, and he stuffed the sandwich into his pocket.

Strangely, Joel did not head in the direction of the squirrel chatter. Instead, he left in the opposite direction.

It was difficult to follow him. He is the master at quiet. I had to stay far enough back so he wouldn't hear me, but close enough so that he couldn't disappear at the blink of an eye.

Somehow, I managed to keep him in sight long enough to find his destination. He reached a tall thick gnarled old tree with knobby branches near the ground and squinted upwards.

I held my breath and crept closer.

Joel took a little jump and hopped onto the lowest branch. He began to climb. Was there a nest up there?

As soon as he disappeared high among the branches, I inched to the tree. It took about five minutes. Then I peered upwards. There was no sight of Joel, but that didn't mean anything. It was a big tree with thick branches for cover.

Before I could decide my next plan of attack, something grabbed me from behind! My arms were pinned together behind me and hands covered my mouth! I nearly fainted for the second time in one day.

"Mmmmppphhh! Mmmmmmmmpppphhhh!"

"If you promise not to yell, we'll let go of your mouth," said a voice. I sagged from relief. It was only Bruce and Jim.

I nodded as vigorously as I could. When I turned my head, I saw that they each had one of my arms.

"Everybody's at the lake," Jim said. "Nobody to help you out of this one."

"Of course, you can always squeal later to a counselor," Bruce said. "But then we'll know you're a real chicken."

I never thought I would be happy to be tied up by those two, but after thinking ghosts and Indian spirits all day, I was nearly overjoyed it was them. Until they took out the honey.

"It's an old Indian trick," Jim said. "Harmless, but fun. We figure we owe you after all the trouble you've caused us. The honey is a nice way to remind you of the antpile you made us sleep in."

"But—"

"First we put honey on your neck and chest. Then we tie you to the tree. Shouldn't be long before ants start crawling all over you."

"Great," I said.

"We'll be back to untie you before the hike starts," said Jim. "Then I think we'll be even."

"Great," I said. I wasn't going to give them the satisfaction of struggling. What really irritated me was knowing it would be hard to think of a trick as good as this one to get them back.

A potato hit Jim on the head. "What was that?"

Another potato hit Bruce on the head. "Ouch." One potato bounced off my shoulder. Suddenly it was raining potatoes, mostly on Jim and Bruce. Any potatoes that hit me sure hurt.

None of us dared look up into the tree to see where the potatoes were coming from. A pan bounced on the ground beside us. Joel! It had to be Joel and yesterday's pans of missing potatoes. How he and the potatoes were in the same tree was a bigger mystery, but one I wasn't going to try to solve just yet. It was enough that he was up there, doing his best to protect me.

"Hey!" Jim shouted angrily as two huge ones clunked on his head. He let go of my left arm. Potatoes kept raining. Another pan clanked down beside us.

Three potatoes bounced off Bruce's head and his grip loosened. The instant that happened, I was gone, tearing straight for our tent.

"Get him, Jim!"

I ran as hard as I could, hoping both Bruce and Jim would chase me. That would give Joel a chance to escape. Potatoes are fine as weapons only as long as you don't run out, and they don't exactly grow in trees.

By the thumping and grunting behind me, I could tell both of them were in hot pursuit. It meant Joel was safe, but I wasn't; I still had to make it to the tent. I had a secret weapon stashed there, one of my emergency preparations for Joel.

"Faster, Jim!" Bruce shouted. I didn't have much of a lead.

I tore through the small clearing near our firepit, reached the tent, and dove inside. I scrambled through my knapsack, found the weapon and got outside again, and stood in front of the tent near the flap. I braced myself for Jim and Bruce.

"Stay back," I said as they skidded into the clearing.

"There's two of us, and only one of you," said Jim. They moved in and I blasted them with my secret weapon.

For a moment, they stared at me. Then they looked at each other and sniffed the air. They stared at me in disbelief, stared at what I held in my hand in disbelief, then stared at each other again.

"Aaaagh!" They both grabbed their faces. It took them less than a second to start complaining. "Yuck. Oh, yuck. How could you do this to us?"

Then they did the last thing I expected. They started laughing. "OK, Ricky Kidd. This is it. You're in big trouble now." It didn't sound so dangerous when they were laughing. I had to laugh with them, too. The emergency preparation all over both of them was getting stronger by the second. Before they could try anything else, there was the sound of nearby voices.

"Next time, Ricky," Bruce said. "Next time, we're really going to get you."

Jim said, "And we'll get your potato-throwing friend in the tree too. It's going to be an interesting camp over the next few days."

Little did we know how right they would be. They scooted into the trees just before Mike and Ralphy came in from the other side.

Ralphy sniffed the air. "What's that smell? My mother isn't here, is she?"

I shook my head, wondering what Bruce and Jim would say to that question. *They* were the ones smelling thickly of perfume.

There are times when there is no way to see or hear Joel as he follows me. I had planned for that by getting the special preparation I've used before for other emergencies—a big bottle of cheap perfume. With it, when he fools my eyes and ears, I could still smell him.

I took the bottle from behind my back and checked its contents. Half full. Enough to keep tabs on Joel. The rest, of course, was making Bruce and Jim very fragrant.

"The air is smelly, isn't it," I said. "You won't believe what happened." I told Ralphy and Mike about being trapped under the tree, how Joel saved me by throwing down potatoes, and how they just missed a perfume fight.

Mike frowned. "If Joel was throwing potatoes from high above you in a tree, and you raced straight here, how come Joel is in the tent behind you?"

I turned around. Joel smiled sweetly at me.

"Was in sleeping bag," Joel said. "How come you make funny smell?"

I could hardly breathe. "If you weren't throwing potatoes, who was? And how did the potatoes get there?"

Joel shrugged and smiled again. I fought off another fainting attack.

15

"OK, Guys, this is a warning!" Counselor Ted shouted. "We're heading back now. Anybody who wants to be upwind of Bruce and Jim should get to the front of the line!"

Everybody giggled. We were at the far edge of the lake, relaxing after a long hike. A few guys had gone swimming, including Bruce and Jim. Actually, the counselors had forced Bruce and Jim into the lake, because the smell of the cheap perfume was so strong. It was fun hearing them wriggle with the excuses they were making for wearing perfume in the middle of a Cadet camp. Unfortunately, I was too worried about the potatoes to really enjoy listening.

As we headed back, Jim caught up to me.

He grinned. "This does mean warfare, you know."

"That's OK," I said. "I haven't had a chance to tell you the scary part. It wasn't any friend of mine throwing potatoes."

"What do you mean?"

"I mean I have no idea who threw those potatoes. In fact, if those were the stolen potatoes, I have no idea how they got into the tree. The rest of the Cadets were at the lake, and Joel was back in the tent. And I didn't have a chance to go back to the tree to check before we left on this hike."

"You don't think . . ." Jim shook his head, trying not to think about it.

"All I know is that things aren't normal at this camp," I said. "Just keep your eyes open."

He nodded, eyes wide.

"One other thing, Jim," I whispered.

"What?" He leaned close to me.

"I still have half a bottle of perfume left."

He had no chance to reply.

"Mr. Vanderhoek!" Two Cadets were further ahead, pointing wildly at something on a tree. It was a Cadet shirt, shredded as if by a giant claw. Thick red liquid dripped from the shirt to the ground. It was stuck into the tree with a grey and red and black painted stick decorated with crow's feathers.

I looked around, wondering if we were going to be attacked. Everyone else thought the same thing, but nothing happened. It was a quiet hike back, and we all walked so close together we could have all been carrying the same knapsack.

Worse, we discovered four more shirts exactly like the first one. They were stuck into trees along our hiking trail. Mr. Vanderhoek collected each one and kept them in his knapsack. Even he looked upset.

It was worse back at the camp, even though we didn't know it at first.

In front of the counselors' cabin most of the camp's pots and pans were set on the ground. Each was filled with garbage.

Around the pots and pans were all the rest of the camp's axes and hatchets. Actually, they were just the heads, charred and black; the handles were burned to crispy splinters. The heads had been carefully pushed into the ground.

"Senior Cadets stay here," Mr. Vanderhoek said. "Counselors, return with your groups to their tents. I want you to check each tent carefully to make sure this camp is safe."

As soon as everybody else left, Mr. Vanderhoek turned to us older Cadets.

"Look closely. Anybody notice anything unusual?"

Mike whistled sharp and low. "Yes. The pattern of the pots and pans. They form a giant tomahawk!"

Mike was right. I stepped back involuntarily. Something sticking out one of the pots caught my eye. "And that garbage belongs to me," I said. "It is one of the comic books that Ralphy was reading before he gave up on the parts the goats ate."

"Goats?" Mr. Vanderhoek said. "Here?"

I shook my head. "It's a long story. But it looks like all the garbage in those pots came from us over the last few days." There were wrappings from the weiner packages and empty juice containers that could have come only from our supplies.

I still hadn't told any of the counselors about the potatoes from the tree. I wanted to check it on my own first. Unfortunately, it was getting too dark to do it right away.

"We'll keep this quiet," Mr. Vanderhoek said. "No sense in scaring the younger Cadets more than they are. If you see anything else unusual, come tell me immediately. But don't broadcast it across the camp or—"

A shout interrupted him. Counselor Ted came running back.

"Dead fish, Mr. Vanderhoek. Some of the Cadets are finding dead fish in their sleeping bags."

Great.

Somehow, camp wasn't becoming my ideal way to spend a summer week.

* * * * * * * *

Most of us Cadets sat in front of the campfire and shivered. It was a warm night, but the day's events were too fresh in our minds. Clouds had moved in and without light from the moon and stars, it was very, very black. It took Mike to break the silence.

"Mr. Vanderhoek, if there really are spirits, how can we fight them?" It was the question on all our minds. We leaned closer to listen.

"Drink hot chocolate, Mike."

Most of us sat back and groaned. It was not the answer we needed.

"Really," Mr. Vanderhoek said. "Drink your hot chocolate. And enjoy it. Can't you believe you're in God's hands?"

"Sure," Mike said. "But even in God's hands, we need to protect ourselves. If I see a mad bear charging, I still need to climb a tree. Drinking hot chocolate wouldn't get me out of that one."

Mr. Vanderhoek laughed. "Absolutely right. The saying is 'God helps those who help themselves.' Against a charging bear you can easily understand the best way to deal with it."

His face became more serious. "This is different. Right now, we don't understand what's happening around us. A solution isn't obvious."

He sipped on his hot chocolate. "It works that way in the rest of life too. Most of the time you know how to solve your problems, even if the solution is difficult to put into action. For example, if you break a window, you know how to make it right. If your marks are low in school, you know you need to study harder or ask for help."

His face grew thoughtful. "The trouble is that some problems don't have clear solutions. As you grow older, you will face questions that don't have easy answers. Maybe career decisions. Or love decisions."

Mr. Vanderhoek paused. It was a long time before he spoke again. "Or whether or not to take a group of scared Cadets back to Jamesville. That's when you need the strength to trust God. When you can't see a solution, all you can really do is pray for wisdom and, in this case, drink hot chocolate."

In the darkness under the black sky it seemed even the creaking of insects stopped in the silence that followed Mr. Vanderhoek's last words.

It was Ralphy who stood up first. "Look, everybody, if I'm gonna be scared, I'm gonna be scared of something I can see. Like outhouses or snakes."

Coming from Ralphy, that was a good one. He continued. "If something is trying to scare us by being sneaky, I say we fight back by staying right here and drinking hot chocolate."

Mike said, "And I'll sew doll's clothes for a living before admitting I'm scared of something that doesn't bother Ralphy!"

Mr. Vanderhoek stood up and laughed until all of us joined him. "Counselor Ted," he roared, "better throw some more milk in the hot chocolate pot. We've got a lot of drinking to do."

It was fun for the next half hour, swapping jokes and telling ghost stories. The scarier the story, the more we laughed. Ralphy topped it off with his best poem yet.

He read it out loud as I shone my flashlight over his shoulder:

In this rime we'll discuss
That famous meat that cauzed a fuss;

It's not as good as chicken
Cuz when you're dunn yer fingers don't kneed licken.

So if you don't know 'Where's the beef?'
Or if your frigerator has been hit by a thief,

Of this I do know what I am
If it's left behind it ain't pork, it's Spam.

Inspiration hit Mike. He shouted, "How's this?"

Where only one meat is left alone where you're looking,
You know it must be counselors' cooking!

Counselor Ted laughed so hard that he spilled hot chocolate
on himself. It made us laugh more. He howled and slapped his
legs where the hot chocolate spilled. With all the noise, it took
a while for us to notice a new noise.

"Oooooooooohhhh! Oooooooooohhhhhh! Ooooooooooohhhhh!"

The noise grew louder. Our laughing died in a hurry.

It came from another direction. "Aaaaaaoooohhhhh!
Aaaaaaoooohhhh!"

Each time the noise started low and built to a loud chilling
moan. I didn't dare move.

From a third direction it came. "Aaaaaaaoooohhhhhh!
Aaaaaaaoooooohhhh! Aaaaaaaooooooohhhhh!" And then from a
fourth direction.

Every single Cadet moved closer to the fire. Even Joel looked
scared.

There was a loud crack behind us. Suddenly a ghostly white
light flared in a cloud of smoke. An Indian warrior stepped
forward and scowled fiercely. His face was painted the same
way mine had been. He jabbed a tomahawk in our direction,
then stepped back and disappeared.

Craaack! On the other side of the campfire, ghostly white
light flared again. Another warrior stepped out of a cloud of
smoke. He didn't move. He just glared at us, arms crossed, and
gradually faded away as the light around him died.

Craaack! again. The howling noises grew louder from all
directions. The warrior who stepped out from the smoke wore a
bear's head. Ferocious teeth gleamed in the ghostly white light.
The rest of the bear, the fur with legs and claws wrapped

around the warrior, was painted with red streaks.

Suddenly the howling stopped. The warrior in the bear disappeared in the smoke. It was deathly quiet. It happened so quickly none of us had moved. Not even Mr. Vanderhoek.

From the black of the night came a light scraping. Ralphy stood and pointed, his face frozen in horror. Floating towards us, above the fire, was yet another spirit.

Ralphy could only move his mouth open and shut. No words came out. We were all paralyzed with fear.

The spirit floated closer and closer above us in the dark night. The slight scraping sound was like bones against bones. It loomed closer and we saw the true horror.

It wasn't a warrior at all. Instead, it was a young Indian boy. Dried blood ran across his face and embedded in his shoulder was a large tomahawk.

It whispered to us in agony. *"Kasa wapa met ima longi! Kasa wapa met ima longi!"* Ten feet above us it stopped and beseeched us with pain in its eyes. *"Met ima loni. Kasa Kasa!"*

That was the last we heard. A mighty roar ripped the air from behind us! We jumped and turned.

A spirit loomed five feet above the ground about twenty yards away. In full headdress, he shook his tomahawk and roared again. *"Yama gula gitchie mae!"* The howling around us built to a feverish pitch. Something in the fire exploded and the flames flared straight up!

We ducked, and the howling stopped as suddenly as it began. The young Indian boy was no longer floating above us and the Indian warrior had disappeared.

As the fire slowly died to its normal height, complete silence surrounded us. Everything had happened within minutes. Now it was as if nothing had happened. The *creak-creak* of insects started humming again. It took five minutes before anyone spoke.

Finally, Mike said, "Tell me you guys are part of my dream and I'm going to wake up in my bed at home."

It was a brave attempt, and it broke the spell that had been cast upon us. Cadets started buzzing with noise and questions. Mr. Vanderhoek let it continue for at least ten minutes.

"Everybody!" he said. "That was the scariest, craziest thing I've ever seen. I have no idea how to explain it or what it meant. However, I want you to realize one thing. Never, not once, were we actually touched or harmed. I think that should tell us something.

"Tonight, the counselors assigned to your groups will sleep with you in your tents. You have nothing to fear. Each counselor will sleep right at the tent flaps and they will alert you if anything happens. OK?"

There was no disagreement. Counselor Ted looked white in the firelight, but he didn't say a word.

"Fine then," Mr. Vanderhoek said. "Stick together as you go back to your tents. Tomorrow we'll decide what to do."

That is how it worked. Each tent had a counselor sleeping at the front. I felt sorry for them.

Not only did they get to do most of the worrying, but every Cadet in camp had drunk double the usual amount of hot chocolate. I'll bet each counselor got tromped on a dozen times. The spirit attack made us wait way past the emergency point before tearing out to go to the bathroom. And when we charged back into the safety of the tent, we ran back in like buffaloes.

16

Even with Counselor Ted sleeping at the front of the tent, the slightest noises were enough to make a Cadet jump. The only person in our tent who slept was Joel.

After breakfast, the counselors called us together by the main campfire. In daylight, it seemed hard to believe we had seen spirits floating above the fire the night before.

"This is a tough time for all of us," Mr. Vanderhoek said right away. "As you know, unexplained events have been happening all around us. The question we face as counselors, Cadets, and Christians is difficult. Do we stay or do we go?"

He paused. It seemed difficult to be afraid while the sun shone so brightly.

"On one hand," he continued, "the safest thing to do is leave. Although these events have seemed threatening, so far no one has been hurt. All of us have a responsibility to protect our friends. Leaving here would do that.

"On the other hand, we must be careful of running away. If we do, each of us will remember that we dealt with something frightening by taking the easy way out. As well, we are Christians. Should we let the unknown frighten us when we believe in God as the One who watches over us? Will running away show that we have no trust in Him? And what kind of example is that to those at home, those who will not understand what we saw last night?"

When a squirrel chattered behind us, no one twitched in temptation.

"Last night I said there are situations that have no clear answers. This is one of them," he said. "Each of you decide for yourselves. Remember, there is no wrong or right."

Mr. Vanderhoek began to hand out small pieces of paper. "Just write 'go' or 'stay,' depending on what you think we should do."

As we shared the pencils among us, it was very quiet. When a Cadet paused to think hard before scratching down an answer, the others were patient. In five minutes Mr. Vanderhoek had all the papers back.

He frowned as he opened the first one. He kept the frown all the way through reading them. When he finished, he looked up gravely.

"This pile of votes says that we should go back to Jamesville," he said quietly. He held out a closed hand, then opened it in front of us. Not one piece of paper fell to the ground.

"Yes," he said. "Each of you decided to remain here. That makes my decision easy."

The nearby squirrel chattered angrily again. Mr. Vanderhoek smiled. "Don't worry, squirrel, you'll have your peace and quiet very soon."

He turned to us. "We leave this afternoon. That's my decision alone. None of you voted to run away. Each of you will take courage back to Jamesville, instead of leaving it behind. If ever you're afraid, remember your decision today."

Mr. Vanderhoek had us join him in a short prayer of gratitude for our safety and joy so far at camp, then he gave us the morning to enjoy our remaining time.

"Have fun, but stay within shouting distance of the camp," he said. "Right after lunch we begin packing."

Just as he said that, a battered old truck wheezed its way to camp and stopped where our bus was parked.

Sheila stepped out of the truck and calmly walked towards the group of us.

"Just taking orders for tomorrow's supplies," she said. "Milk, fresh bread, or—" she searched for my face—"makeup. Any takers?"

"Makeup?" Mike muttered.

"Forget it," I said. Sheila, I was sure, was about to laugh at our group's decision.

"Sorry," Mr. Vanderhoek said. "We're leaving today. But please thank your father for all his help with supplies."

"OK." That was all she said. I thought I saw a smirk, but she turned back to the truck too quickly.

Why did her reaction make me uneasy?

* * * * * * * *

If it was my last morning at camp, I was determined to take a look at that gnarled old tree. Without being spied on by Joel.

Mike wanted to do some fishing, since he hadn't caught anything yet. Ralphy agreed to keep an eye on Joel for the morning, but I knew better. Joel would give him the slip after half an hour and begin something much more satisfying, namely, spying on me. So I went to one of my last emergency preparations, the fake sleeping trick.

As we walked back to our tent, I yawned. "Ralphy, while you and Joel are down at the lake, I'm going to nap. I didn't sleep much last night."

The last thing I had purchased to deal with Joel was a

leftover Halloween wig. As he and Ralphy went down to the lake, I dug it out of my knapsack. I filled my sleeping bag with clothes so it would look like a body, then covered most of the wig with the top of the sleeping bag. In the dim light of the tent, it looked exactly like I was snuggled inside. When Joel escaped Ralphy to see if I was sleeping, he would be fooled completely.

I went the long way to the gnarled tree. The first thing I noticed was that the potatoes were gone from the ground. That was strange, because the tree wasn't near any paths, and I doubted any Cadets or counselors had been nearby since the day before.

Without waiting, because I knew if I thought about it I would get scared, I began to climb the tree. It was a thick tree, nearly as wide as our tent, and it was as easy as going up a ladder.

The tree was scarred with age. Old gashes and marks showed where branches had broken or insects and birds had damaged the bark. Halfway up, just before the tree started to narrow, there was a large hole in its side, big enough to store pots of potatoes. It was empty, though, except for some strands of steel wire.

I sat on the branch near the hole and thought. As hard as I tried, I could come up with no reason for anybody or anything to steal potatoes and keep them in a tree away from everything. And why the short pieces of steel wire?

Below me, I could hear Cadets' voices around the camp almost as if they were right under the tree. It was a pretty good spot for seeing most of the camp. Not too far away was our main campfire spot where we had drunk the hot chocolate.

I puzzled long and hard, but didn't come up with anything. I stood to stretch because the branch was thick and strong and it was safe high up there in the tree. After a good yawn, I turned back to the tree. Safe or not, it was a good idea to hold it securely as I climbed down. I nearly jumped. It seemed like a thousand bugs were gathering around fresh sap dripping from a narrow groove around the bark. There was another tiny hole filled with more sap and bugs.

Great.

Instead of solving anything, I was about to become a new home for ugly bugs.

It was time to get down and see if Mike had caught any fish. Maybe he could make sense of all of this.

17

Halfway to the lake, I nearly stumbled across a fawn. It was impossible to see. Its fur was dappled. With the sun shining across the leaves and branches that covered the fawn, I was lucky not to step on it. It got up slowly and bounced away about ten feet. The fawn was the height of a large dog, but it was so skinny I wondered how it could survive alone for any time at all.

Where was the mother? I looked hard and saw nothing. I guess with all the noise and Cadets around, any mother deer would be scared to stay nearby. I couldn't leave the fawn alone to be hurt by some animal in the woods.

Later, Mr. Vanderhoek explained to me that fawns can take care of themselves quite well. Sometimes the mother will leave to do some feeding, but they never lose each other. Unfortunately, I was too eager to be a hero and save a fawn that didn't need saving.

It wasn't too scared of me. Every time I stepped closer, it only bounced away one or two hops. The more it moved, the more I knew I had to catch it. After all, it was getting farther and farther from its mother.

"Come here, little fella. I won't hurt you. I just want to keep you from bad things in the woods."

Holding out tender juicy grass didn't seem to tempt the fawn, so I kept following it. Once I nearly got close enough to touch it. It quivered a bit, then bounced away. Boy, did it need my help. After all, we were probably a mile from where it first was lost.

It hardly seemed like five minutes of chasing the fawn, but when I looked at my watch, it was 11:00. An hour had passed. That gave me a chill. Suddenly I noticed how deep the woods were. It was pretty quiet, too.

"Look, Pal," I said. "Enough of this. I gotta get back and you do too. Your mother is probably going crazy."

As if to agree, the fawn suddenly darted into the bush. After all its slow bouncing, I was surprised to see how strong it was. I forgot all about being gentle and slow, and dashed after it. I didn't have a chance. I saw an occasional flash of white as it lifted its tail, but by the time I lost my breath from running, I also lost the fawn.

"Is that gratitude?" I said to the woods. "See if I offer babysitting services to any other animals this week."

That reminded me that I should find Ralphy and see if he was surviving Joel. I headed back to camp.

At least I thought I was heading back to camp. Nothing looked familiar as I walked, but that didn't surprise me. Concentrating on the fawn had been hard work, and I hadn't watched where I was going.

I looked at my watch again. It was noon already! The Cadets would be starting to take down their tents about now. I sat on a log and listened for Cadet noises. If it had been an hour following the fawn, an hour's worth of walking back should have me right near the camp.

It is hard to believe how quiet the woods can be when you start to worry that you might be lost. I had no idea where I was.

A branch snapped somewhere nearby. I told myself it was nothing.

It is also hard to believe how much it can feel like a thousand eyes are watching you when you realize you are lost in the woods. I undid my hatchet from its pouch on my belt and held it in my right hand. Another branch snapped.

I began walking as quietly as I could. Right then, it didn't matter which direction I went, just as long as I got away from the mysterious branch snapping.

Wolves, I told myself, were really as shy as all the wilderness books said. Bears didn't follow people, right? Cougars, I reminded myself, were a rare species, but suddenly I didn't feel sorry for them like I used to when I was reading about them in the Jamesville library. What else was big enough to be dangerous?

Not spirits. Hah. Spirits couldn't hurt people. They could only make noise and scare you. Another branch snapped. I walked quicker.

Somewhere I had read that you shouldn't run. That only makes things chase you.

I walked so fast I almost got dizzy. I had to stop for breath, but I didn't want to breathe because it made too much noise and I couldn't hear if anything was sneaking up on me.

Then I told myself that it was crazy, thinking that I was being spied on. Branches snapped in the woods all the time. Something to do with freak air currents and the way the moon affected gravity. Of course.

I relaxed.

Something rustled in the bushes behind me. *That was enough.*

I ran as fast as I could. It didn't matter where, but I was putting distance between me and the thing behind me making noises. I was so scared I forgot the camper's cardinal rule about never running with a hatchet in your hand.

"Aaaarghhh—"

Thump! I tripped over a root and went flying into a bramble bush. I landed face forward so that my nose was almost buried. It hurt so bad being prickled I wanted to scream. Instead, I only made small choking noises in my throat. Maybe the thing behind me wouldn't notice me lying in a heap in a bramble bush.

A branch snapped again. My hatchet had flown out of my hand into the trees ahead of me. I couldn't move and it even hurt to make the choking noises in my throat. Two more branches snapped. It wasn't my imagination! Something had been following me!

There was only one thing to do. Fake being dead. I couldn't bear to look behind me to see what it was, in case it made me faint. I somehow managed to stop the quivers of my pain.

I could feel the presence of something behind me. I squinted my eyes shut. It rustled forward and paused. The tension made me want to whimper, but somehow I muffled it.

Forward it moved slowly. *OK,* I thought, *jump on me now and get it over with.*

Something brushed my shoulder. It took every ounce of strength I had not to move. The tension built and built. Whatever it was backed away. I couldn't take it much longer, but I had to. I hadn't been chomped yet, so faking death was working.

My nerves were so stretched I wanted to cry and scream and laugh at the same time. I stayed frozen, though. I stayed that way for five minutes. Every second of the five minutes was an hour of agony.

Nothing moved behind me. Finally, I could stand it no more. Not moving was killing me. I preferred to be killed quickly by the ferocious beast behind me instead of slowly killing myself.

It cost me another hundred scratches to jump up and shoot forward for my hatchet. Somehow I grabbed it and whirled around in one motion.

Sitting on a log just behind the bramble bush was Joel. He looked at me quizzically and pulled his teddy bear in a little closer.

I managed to sit down before I fainted.

"Where's Ralphy?" I asked half hopefully. Joel shrugged. It was a dumb question anyway. If Ralphy were nearby, he would be in just as much trouble as we were.

There was no doubt. We were lost. At first I was mad at Joel for scaring me. Then I was happy with him for being with me. Then I was mad again because he had gotten lost too.

I didn't know what to do. Sure, the survival books explained how to walk in one direction without going in circles. You simply sight on any landmark—a hill, tall tree, or some rocks. When you get there, look back at the last landmark you used and line up both landmarks to point to a third one ahead of you.

Simple. Except the survival books didn't explain how to choose your direction in the first place. Walking in a straight line wasn't much good if it took you in the opposite direction of where you needed to go.

At least worrying was making me forget about the brambles sticking into me.

"Great," I said. "The rest of camp is packing up, and we're stuck in the middle of nowhere with nothing but a teddy bear."

He shrugged again and smiled at his teddy bear.

I tried remembering maps I had seen of the area. Some roads ran through the woods and there were a lot of creeks. With luck, we would find one that led to Lake Blackeagle.

"Come on, Joel. We have to find our way back before anyone begins to worry."

A brainstorm hit me. "Joel, do you know how to get back?"

He grinned shyly and shook his head. It showed my respect for his spying abilities that I expected him to know.

"We lost?" he asked.

"Hah!" I said. "Never. Follow me."

Five hours later, I decided maybe Lake Blackeagle wasn't so easy to find.

"Joel, if you decide to disappear now, I'll hunt you down and strangle your teddy bear." I wasn't in the mood to be lost alone.

The counselors were probably frantic. With everyone else packed and ready to go, what would they do? I sat down to think.

Joel sat down beside me.

"OK, Joel, think. If we aren't back at camp, what will they do?"

He shrugged, still happy.

"They'll start a small search party first," I said. "By now, they'll decide we might seriously be lost. They'll probably go back to the general store to get help. I just hope they don't call Mom or Dad. After all, we're perfectly safe, aren't we, Joel?"

Back in Jamesville, I always thought being lost would be a great adventure. Living off the land and coolly showing up at the last minute.

It was a lot different in real life.

Too soon we had been lost for seven hours. The sun was setting as the air became cooler. I figured there was only an hour or so of light to go. Decision time. Keep looking for camp, or get ready for the night?

An owl hooted from the darkening trees. Joel jumped in delight. I shivered with fear. The owl was enough of an answer for me. It was time to get as secure as possible. I sure hoped building a fire would be as easy. In camp, at least, we had plenty of paper to use as starter.

I showed Joel the type of tiny, dry branches we needed. Fortunately, I found a birch tree nearby. Birch trees have an oily thick bark which peels easily and burns like a torch.

After Joel had gathered enough tiny branches, I sent him looking for larger ones. I kept his teddy bear as insurance. While he was getting wood, I measured the distance between two trees and found a long, skinny piece of wood to fit between the two.

I was glad for my hatchet. With it I managed to carve horizontal grooves on the front of both trees, about three feet up the trunks. I laid the long, skinny pole into the grooves and tied it tight with some string from my survival kit. Next, I cut some wide boughs from spruce trees. I rested the top of the boughs against the beam and piled them across from one end to the other to make a temporary lean-to. It wouldn't stop bears, wolves, or moose, which I hated to think about, but it would stop most rain and wind.

Joel returned with his third armful of branches. I told him to rest and went out for the thick logs myself. In about half an hour, there was nearly enough for the night.

"Okay, Joel, cross your fingers." I scraped a fire pit with the back end of my hatchet. First I laid down the pieces of birch bark. Above that a network of tiny branches. Nearby I had some middle-sized pieces.

My survival kit sure looked puny. But at least it had matches. The bark caught right away and flared into a bright flame. Almost immediately the small branches began burning. I gently fed the medium-sized branches into the flames.

"It's going to work, Joel. If we keep this fire burning all night, we'll be okay." He smiled happily and rubbed his hands in front of the flames.

I had to pretend everything was okay, too. If Joel knew I was scared, it wouldn't be fun for him anymore.

"It's a good time for hot chocolate, Kid," I said. Joel thought I meant for drinking and nodded. But I was thinking of what Mr. Vanderhoek said about trusting in God. That helped me.

In the light of the flames, I prowled around our little campsite, carefully trimming the soft buds at the ends of the boughs of spruce trees. Sleeping right on the ground would suck the warmth from our bodies. The tips of the boughs made a mattress that was better than nothing.

"Suppertime, Joel." I was glad for the two granola bars that were part of my survival kit. Even though we were both still hungry after, it was better than nothing.

In the darkness, I fed another log into the fire and sat back. Joel, of course, had his teddy bear tight in his arms.

"When go back?" he asked.

His quiet trust nearly made me cry. I usually forget he is my younger brother and that he sometimes needs me. Mostly he is so stubborn and independent, he'll do the opposite of anything I say or want. In fact, he usually terrified me with his ways of sneaking like a ghost.

I snapped my fingers. Ghosts! Something that had been bugging me all day about the potato tree clicked. How could I have missed the obvious? Fresh sap and strands of steel wire could only mean one thing.

Joel nearly jumped at my snapping fingers. "Sorry, Joel. We'll go back tomorrow. I promise." There would be time to think about the ghosts later.

When the first hint of light crept through the trees, I was cold and stiff and ready to start looking for camp again. Even though it was Friday morning, it felt like we had been lost forever.

"Joel, wake up." Naturally, he was nestled in the spruce boughs and sleeping soundly. Nothing frightens him.

"Where is camp?" he asked.

"I don't know," I said. The lack of sleep made me grouchy. I waved my arms in a circle to point at all the trees and snapped, "Can you see it from here?"

He shook his head. Then his eyes snapped wide open. "Climb tree and look?"

"Aaaaaaggghhh." I could have smacked myself. "Of course. From the highest tree I might be able to spot the lake."

It turned out even better. The sun was high enough so that the entire sky was white with morning. I climbed to the top of a huge tree and saw smoke rising in a gray-brown line about two miles away. "Camp, Joel! I see the camp! We're not lost after all!"

I nearly fell through the branches three times, I was in such a hurry to reach the ground. It didn't matter. We were safe.

I lined up the next largest tree in the direction of the camp and we marched towards it. Five minutes later, I lined up another tree. Every fifteen minutes I climbed a tall tree to make sure we were going in the right direction. I did not want to risk getting lost again.

"By the way, Joel," I said. "I have to admit that was a great idea about going up a tree to look for the camp."

He was behind me and didn't reply, which didn't surprise me. I had his teddy bear, so I knew he wouldn't stray.

Instead, he made a small whimpering sound.

It sent a chill up my spine. Something about a noise of fright coming from Joel had to be serious. I spun around to help him.

A small woofing noise came from the bushes we had just walked through. Ice gripped me, even though I had never heard that sound before. I knew, even before it swung its massive head through the bushes, what it was.

There it stood. A huge, shaggy bear. It was close enough that I could have thrown a baseball the distance from second plate to home and hit it squarely in the nose. It made that small woofing noise again. That was the worst sound I have ever heard in my life.

The bear was black and had shoulders the size of a horse. Its eyes glittered through the fur on its face. It swung its head from side to side, testing the air. When it opened its mouth to snap at a fly, the loud click of teeth slamming together made every muscle in my body flinch.

The bear grunted in irritation at Joel and me.

I spend a lot of time being scared and hiding it, especially with a brother as terrifying as Joel, and a friend who can get in as much trouble as Mike. That kind of trouble, though, was all kid's stuff, and the instant the bear grunted, I knew it. It made me a lot older in a big hurry.

This was serious business. If that bear charged, there would be no Mom or Dad or counselors to make it better or lecture us for getting into trouble.

I only had time to pray, "God help us." The bear took a step forward and that somehow drove all the fear and wondering out of my mind.

I spoke in a low voice. It was a mean, hard voice Joel had never heard from me. "Joel, behind me, now. Get behind me and slowly walk to a tree. Climb the tree no matter what happens here. And stay in the tree all day." I hissed, "Do it now!"

Joel moved without hesitating. I think he was more scared of me than the bear. For once I was glad he could move so quietly. The bear stood up on two legs and glared suspiciously. It blocked out the sky.

Ten seconds later, it snorted loudly and took one step forward.

"God," I prayed aloud, "please give me the strength not to run away. Please protect my brother Joel."

The bear paced ahead one more step. It was not in a hurry. I gritted my teeth and tried to keep my feet still. Was Joel in a tree yet? I couldn't look.

Another small woof. The bear rose again to sniff the air. I moved a tiny step back.

Two more steps closer by the bear. It was only the distance from the pitching mound to home plate. I slowly reached down for my hatchet, but stopped. It would be useless against the monstrous bear.

Yesterday, I had been terrified to the breaking point when I didn't know what was in the bushes. Now, with the bear in front of me, instead of being scared, I felt like a faraway observer of what was happening to me. Funny, huh?

The bear began another step toward me, then stopped.

From almost beside me, an old Indian glided out of the bushes to stand between me and the bear. The old Indian and the bear stared at each other.

"Yama gula gitchie mae," the old man said softly. "Leave the little one alone."

The bear hesitated. It swung its head low to the ground.

"Yama gula gitchie mae," the old man said. He murmured a stream of low, soothing syllables in a voice without fear and with quiet authority. "Go now," he finally said to the bear.

It rose on two feet and hung against the sky. When it dropped to the ground an eternity later, it turned and padded into the bushes.

It was as if a bear had never been there. "Thank you," I said.

I didn't realize tears were streaming down my face until the old Indian took a cloth from the pocket of his faded blue jeans and wiped my cheeks.

"It's OK now," he said. "The bear just had to know you were both children of the woods. He is gone."

"Joel," I tried calling, but my voice was a croak. I sat on a log and did not move. Joel came forward and held my hand. The old Indian gave me as much time as I needed to feel strong again.

"I'm ready now," I said. "My brother and I need to get back to camp. Our friends will be worried about us."

"I will take you there," the old Indian said.

We followed his sure footsteps through the woods. I didn't say much. I was still stunned from the fear of the bear and the sudden way we were saved.

Finally, I asked, "How did you happen to be there?"

The old Indian chuckled. "I discovered you early at your lean-to, just before the sun rose. I wanted to give you the chance to earn your own way back to camp. I would do the same for my sons."

We walked a little further. "You discovered us early? Does

that mean you were looking for us?"

"Yes. All night. We had heard you were missing."

"We?"

"My sons and I. I have five," he said proudly. "Between us, we had a good chance of finding you. We have lived in this area all our lives."

Something bothered me as we walked. I could not decide what it was, but it circled inside my head like a fly.

"What is your name?" I asked the old Indian.

"Fred."

"Oh." I had been expecting something different.

He chuckled. "However, I have an Indian name. Kasawapamat. It means 'one who sees.'"

That was more like it. Joel tromped faithfully behind us. I could not place the thought that was tickling my mind. Ahead, we heard noises. Camp noises! It was hard not to run.

The old Indian brought us to the edge of the camp.

"Thank you again," I said. Joel nodded fiercely in agreement.

The old Indian shook my hand gravely. "No. Thank you, fearless one. It was good to see such bravery in front of the bear. If you keep what happened inside you, and tell no one of the way you stood strong, the bravery will grow and help you many times. You now have an Indian name. 'Shee-wap,' the bear warrior."

I struggled for something to say.

Suddenly, the quiet morning air was shattered with shouts.

"Ricky! Joel! Hey everybody, they're back!"

Mike and Ralphy came running up. They ran so hard they had to rest by leaning on their knees and panting for breath.

"So, uh, it's good to see you," Mike said.

"We weren't worried," Ralphy said. "Not for a second."

Playing it cool, were they?

"Neither was I," I said.

I remembered the old Indian. "Especially when Fred here showed up to help us back." I turned to smile at the old Indian. He was gone.

Mike laughed. "Fred? Are you making up stories?" For a second, I thought I had. The old Indian had vanished more quietly than Joel ever could.

"Forget it," I said.

"Anything exciting happen?" Mike asked.

I looked behind me at the wall of trees the Indian had taken us through. "Nothing worth talking about," I said.

* * * * * * * *

"Six-thirty in the morning?" Mr. Vanderhoek looked at his watch. "I thought I told you two that we were leaving yesterday afternoon."

Joel and I hung our heads. The counselors were drinking coffee in the kitchen cabin.

He smiled. "I don't know whether to hang you or hug you. What happened? Are you OK?"

"A little tired," I said. I explained how we had become lost and how long a night can seem deep in the woods.

"Tell me about it," Counselor Ted said. "It wasn't easy for us. We spent hours in groups looking for you. Mr. Vanderhoek went to the general store and got more help." He looked at Mr. Vanderhoek. "I'll head back there now and tell everybody it's OK."

"Good, Ted. And phone Ricky's mom and dad. They'll be glad to hear the news."

"I'm sorry," I said. Joel nodded his head morosely.

"I'm sorry, too," Mr. Vanderhoek said. "A lot of people were nervous. But it's happened, we can't change it, and it's very, very good to have you back safe and sound."

He explained that it took until they were just about ready to leave before anyone noticed we were gone. Ralphy assumed Joel was with me. Mike assumed Ralphy knew where I was. Both figured I was just too lazy to help pack. Once the counselors knew we were lost, they started search parties.

"Did you know about an old Indian looking for us?" I asked.

Mr. Vanderhoek frowned in thought and shook his head. "No," he said. "That's news to me. When it got too dark, we could only sit and wait."

I grinned, thinking of the last campfire. "And drink hot chocolate," I said.

The last campfire! Suddenly, the thought that had circled through my head ran into a brick wall. A lot of things that had been tugging at the corners of my mind fell into place.

"I'll bet a million dollars that no spirits showed up last night to haunt you," I said.

"You'd win the bet, Ricky. What makes you say that?"

Instead of answering, I asked, "Are you still planning that the Cadets leave here as soon as possible instead of waiting until it finishes tomorrow?"

"This camp hasn't exactly been our best one," he said. "And worse things may happen tonight."

"If Mike and Ralphy and Joel and I solve the mystery of the Indian spirits, will it make up for us getting lost?"

Mr. Vanderhoek considered it. "No." He smiled. "But it would come close."

"We have to stay another night." I explained why.

20

I was nervous as it got dark that night. The main campfire was going. It was surrounded by most of the Cadets drinking hot chocolate. Jokes and stories were told a little louder than usual. Everyone there laughed at even the dumbest joke because they were trying hard not to think about what had happened at night around this camp. Even though no spirits had visited the night before, they were hard to forget.

I was worried about the Indian spirits for a different reason. What if they didn't show? Tonight was the last night for us to solve the mystery.

The hot chocolate tasted great, though, especially when I remembered the night before. That made me think of the old Indian.

I pictured his face and told myself again that I really had seen it before. I added up everything I had learned over the last few days, and told myself it could only mean one thing. If the spirits arrived and I was wrong, though, it was going to be a much worse night than being lost.

The moon went behind a cloud and I starting watching

around us very carefully.

The sounds came first.

"Ooooooohhhh! Ooooooooohhhhhhh! Ooooooooooohhhhhh!"

I jumped, even though I had been waiting for it. It came from another direction, just like the time before. "Aaaaaooooohhh! Aaaoooooohhhh!"

Every Cadet moved closer to the fire and looked around in fear. The sounds came from all directions and grew louder and louder. Even though I suspected something different than spirits, it still made my skin crawl.

A loud crack exploded in front of us. The ghostly white light flared and an Indian warrior stepped forward and scowled in rage. The howling grew louder. Two more warriors appeared in full battle dress from the other side of the fire!

When the howling stopped without warning, I listened very carefully for the scraping of bone against bone. There it was!

A few Cadets moaned. I didn't blame them. The scraping got louder and closer. We all crouched and looked up. When would the dying young Indian boy appear?

We saw motion above us. We were so quiet the scraping sound sounded like a roar. If I was right about everything, this was the moment. I didn't dare look. The body of the spirit moved closer and closer until it broke into the light of the fire.

"Hi, guys. How's the hot chocolate?" Ralphy asked as he floated into sight above our heads. He waggled his arms like he was flying and grinned at us.

Behind us in the darkness, someone grunted loudly, "Huh?" and then there was the loud cracking sound. We all turned in time to see the other spirit, the one who floated five feet off the ground. It had a puzzled look on its face.

Into the ghostly white light around the spirit came a curving gush of water. *Splash!* The white light fizzled abruptly. The spirit toppled forward and hit the ground with a thump. Before it could move, Bruce and Jim leaped forward and pounced on it.

Ralphy continued floating above us. "See you later, Guys," he said as he moved forward. He threw something into the fire. Three seconds later, the fire flared sky-high and Ralphy seemed to disappear.

I stood and yelled into the darkness. "Mike and Joel! Come on back to the fire. Bring your friend with you."

I shouted in all other directions. "And the rest of you ghosts might as well come in for hot chocolate too! We have a couple of your brothers."

I paused, enjoying the next words I could shout into the darkness. "And you might as well join us too, Sheila!"

21

They all arrived at the same time. Mike and Joel showed up
with a boy barely bigger than Ralphy. He had a tomahawk taped
to his shoulder with clear Scotch Tape. Red paint was daubed
on his face and shoulder to look like blood.

Bruce and Jim brought in their captive spirit. Makeup was
streaked down his face where the water had soaked him. They
also brought in the stilts he had been standing on.

From the darkness, three other "spirits" slowly shuffled into
the firelight. Their faces were still painted as warriors.

Finally Sheila drifted toward the campfire. She grinned shyly
at me. The contrast was so strong, after seeing her angry most
of the time, that I couldn't stop from grinning in return.

I might still be there, grinning, she looked so cute with that
smile, except Mike elbowed me in the ribs.

Then everybody started talking at once. Mr. Vanderhoek
stopped it right away.

"Hello, spirits, whoever you are. Don't be afraid. We mean
you less harm than you meant us."

Altogether, there were five of them. The biggest one looked

about 17 years old. The smallest one was the one Mike and Joel had caught. In each of their faces, even with the paint, I could see the image of their father, the old Indian who had saved me and Joel from the bear.

They still didn't say anything.

Mr. Vanderhoek said. "If you wish to leave, go ahead. None of us will stop you."

They started to walk away in silence. Mr. Vanderhoek continued. "But then you'll always wonder how you got caught."

They kept walking until they reached the edge of the darkness where Sheila was still standing and smiling.

I'm sure they meant to keep leaving. Then Sheila laughed. She laughed hard for at least two minutes.

When she stopped, she said to her friends, "Hey, you turkeys! Admit it. We got outslicked by a city slicker."

Her grin grew bigger and bigger as she looked across the fire. "And I, for one, am not too proud to want to know how he did it."

The biggest one of the five smacked his forehead. "Oh, nuts!" he said. "I suppose we will have to know. I'd hate to have *you* guys haunting *us* with a mystery."

His brothers gathered behind him and Sheila as they waited from a distance.

"Not so easy." Mr. Vanderhoek smiled. "First, you enjoy our hospitality."

They trooped back to the fire and patiently waited as Counselor Ted found them mugs for hot chocolate. When everybody was settled, Mr. Vanderhoek turned to me.

"Go ahead, Ricky. You explain."

Before I could start, I was interrupted by shouts for help. We all jumped up. Then Mike and I started laughing. The noise belonged to Ralphy.

"Mike, can you help him?" I asked. He grinned and left.

I told them what I knew.

It had started with the potato tree. When I first noticed the bugs in the sap, I didn't think anything of it. Later, lost with Joel, when I remembered that the sap had been fresh, I realized that the grooved line around the tree wasn't made by a bird or animal. It was more like a line left by a tight cable, which explained the strands of steel wire I found.

That part had puzzled me until much later.

The rest of the clues came from the old Indian after the bear attack. At the time, they didn't mean much because I was still in shock. After, I remembered what he had said to the bear—*yama gula gitchie mae.* The spirits haunting us Wednesday night around the campfire had also said it, though in a much different tone of voice.

Then there was the old Indian's face. It had seemed so familiar, but I didn't place it until I closed my eyes to remember the Indian spirits around the fire. Even with the warpaint the resemblance was there. *Why?* I had asked myself.

When the old Indian told me he had five sons, it became more clear. If they truly were not spirits, who else could they be but his sons? And thinking back, I could remember four spirits around the fire, and one in the air. Five sons. It added up.

So when he mentioned his sons had also been searching for me and Joel, I guessed that the camp hadn't been haunted that same night. They were busy elsewhere.

The cable bothered me, though. *Why a cable?* Then I remembered the view from high up in the old gnarled tree. The main campfire was in plain sight. I decided if there was a cable from it to another tree, someone could easily use it to cross above the fire. That theory fit, especially when I climbed a tree opposite across our campfire site and found similar grooved lines around its trunk. And that's what had been the first solid clue to help.

I looked around the campfire as the flames sent dappled light across all the faces. I began by telling them about all the clues. "Mike and Ralphy helped piece all of it together," I said. "The first thing we decided was that it was people scaring us, not spirits. So there was much less to fear. We didn't know all the details, but we knew enough to have a good idea of how to ambush you. Mike and Joel and Ralphy hid near the tree with the cable grooves and waited."

Mike and Ralphy walked up to the campfire. Ralphy had a sheepish look on his face.

"We still didn't know how you crossed on the cable," I said. "But Mike decided if we did capture a spirit, there was no reason we couldn't cross the cable the same way. Right, Ralphy?"

He nodded and turned around. Strapped across his back was a pulley. He held another one in his hand. "This pulley goes on your feet. You run the cable through both pulleys," he explained, mentioning he had caught the youngest "spirit" getting ready to strap it on. "That way you can hang upside down and slowly roll down the cable, making that scraping sound." He frowned. "Only at the end of my ride I got stuck at the end of the cable."

Even the Indian boys laughed.

I continued. "At the same time, Bruce and Jim were waiting in the dark with a bucket of water. They're famous around here for throwing water on people. We figured if spirits were going to haunt us like the time before, one would appear at each corner of the fire in the same way. Bruce and Jim picked a side and waited.

"Somehow, our plan worked. But I have questions. Like how did you get that cable across the trees at night without us noticing?"

"It wasn't easy," the oldest Indian boy, introducing himself as

George, said. "We've had practice, though. Sam, my brother here, is an expert with a bow and arrow. He would stand in one tree and wait until it was nearly dark. You guys never showed up at the main campfire until later anyway.

"Sam tied a light string to an arrow and shot it across the space into the other tree. Someone would climb the other tree and grab the string. Sam then tied his end to the cable and the other person reeled it in with the string."

"Not bad," Mr. Vanderhoek said. "What about the smoke and light you guys stepped through?"

The second oldest Indian, quietly calling himself John, searched through a pocket. He held out some capsules. "Tiny flares that magicians use. I get them in town when I go to school in the winter. Some give light. Some give smoke. What they do is distract the eyes, especially when it's dark."

Mike said, "That explains how you could appear and disappear. By showing up from different directions, you never let us look long enough in one spot to even guess you weren't real spirits."

The boy nodded. "It took some timing, but we've had practice. Bill, our youngest brother, dropped some flares into the fire after he passed over. With flames shooting up like that, eyes can't adjust to the sudden darkness afterwards, giving all of us time to clear out."

"What about the noise?" I asked.

"Easy," Tony, the last Indian, said. "Cassette players hidden in the trees. We begin the tapes with five minutes of blank tape. That way we can start them playing, but get a few minutes to move into position before the howling starts. Scary, huh?"

I nodded. "Then while we city kids are sleeping, all of you go back and clean up the evidence, right? The dead flares, the cable, the speakers in the trees."

George grinned.

I struggled with my next question. "What does *yama gula gitchie mae* mean?"

Sam said, "Go away, you are giving trouble."

"Before I go," I said with a grin, "I want to know who painted my face. That wasn't nice at all."

Sheila was watching all of our conversation in silence. I had guesses about her part in this too.

All of the Indian boys laughed in a mixture of throaty chuckles. Finally Sam recovered his breath enough to speak. "All of us. We had dares going that night to see who could paint the longest without waking you up. The hardest part was not falling out of the spying tree with laughter the next morning. If you could have watched yourself faint when you looked in the mirror!"

I looked at Sheila. "You too?" I asked. "You were in on the painting, weren't you?"

She grinned.

"I thought so."

John broke in, "It was also funny seeing the small one there run away from the stream when he ran into me by accident." He pointed at Ralphy.

"Great," I said. "Still, you guys slipped up by throwing potatoes from that tree. It was the first clue."

Sheila said, "That was my fault. I felt sorry for you."

"Let me guess," I said. "It was your job to spy on us during the daytime. If anyone caught you, you could say you were here for your father. And even if they didn't believe you, at least no one would suspect you were an Indian, or an Indian spirit."

She nodded. "I spent a lot of time in that tree watching all of you guys. Your little brother, who's quieter than any Indian I ever met, knew something was up the tree. He started climbing, heard you, and changed his mind and disappeared. I mean just disappeared. Then those two guys grabbed you as you were looking up the tree."

Mr. Vanderhoek said, "Which two guys?"

"Just a game we were playing," I said quickly, then changed the subject. "But why potatoes up there?"

"I was the one who raided them," Sheila said. "We were going to throw them at you at night if the haunting didn't work. My mistake was deciding two against one wasn't fair, so I unloaded them to help you out."

She shook her head. "Otherwise you would never have guessed. And I wouldn't have to apologize for calling you a city slicker."

Before she could say anything else, her friend George paused and his eyebrows furrowed. "What were chocolate bars doing on the end of a string in the middle of the woods? They tasted great, but it made no sense to us."

I coughed and shrugged.

Mr. Vanderhoek had been quiet for some time. He spoke at last. "This all seems like good fun, except for a couple of things. You terrified us, not only with the haunting, but with the blood-stained shirts, which I assume was chicken blood. You also ruined every ax in this camp. And you say you've had practice. I think that deserves an explanation."

George stopped smiling. He thought for a few seconds, then became angry.

"Yes, it was chicken blood. And I'll tell you why we did this," he said. "It's because we love our land. It hurts us to watch people come in and treat it so badly.

"Why did we burn the axes? The air was never quiet with the chopping of trees. But there was no purpose to destroy trees. The land didn't need clearing. Buildings didn't need building. No, chopping was for the fun of it."

There was embarrassed silence around the fire. Sam spoke next. "The same with animals; why terrorize innocent squirrels? And garbage. We find it thrown all over the woods. We watch campers pour soap and filth into the water. Even to destroy an antpile for no reason. How can that be respect for the land?"

Sheila said quietly. "We live nearby. Each summer this happens as people from outside come to this camp. We wanted it to stop. We knew of the old legend. So we haunted the camp. With practice, we became quite good."

Nobody spoke. The good humor of trading secrets had disappeared. All five Indian boys stood to leave. Sheila placed her hand on the oldest boy's arm to stop him, but he shook it off.

Mr. Vanderhoek stopped them by saying, "Next year, we return anyway."

George scowled. "Next year, we try something different. And worse."

The air was filled with tension. Mr. Vanderhoek ignored George's hard, angry scowl. "These Cadets learned plenty from you tonight. Next year, we will be here to clean up and teach new Cadets how to respect the land."

George crossed his arms and scowled harder. Two of his brothers quickly whispered in his ear. George then looked thoughtful. The silence grew heavier while we waited for his reply. He said, "In that case, we'll definitely be here to do something different next year."

Mr. Vanderhoek and George stared at each other without flinching.

"Yes," George said. "Next year we'll give canoe lessons. Boy, some of you need help." All his brothers started giggling.

Epilogue

"Did you miss me?" Lisa Higgins asked in front of church, the Sunday after we returned.

"Sure," I grinned. "Who wouldn't miss someone who hits home runs off their best pitches."

I wasn't going to tell her that after drinking hot chocolate with all the Indian spirits, I had reminded Sheila that she had been interrupted before she could apologize for calling me a city slicker. I certainly wasn't going to tell Lisa that Sheila's eyes had danced with laughter as she gravely apologized and surprised me with a kiss on the forehead. And I most certainly wasn't going to mention that the spot on my forehead still felt nicely warm when I thought of it.

With Lisa smiling the way she was, I wanted to be a hero for as long as I could.

"See you after church," she said. "You can tell me all about it. Especially the part about moonlight apologies."

She swung her skirt and walked inside, whistling merrily at the redness of my face.

Who else but Mike would have told her?

He was probably still mad about his buried treasure. Could I help it that he was in such a hurry to get it, he jumped into the Bradleys' backyard without checking the doghouse first? The German shepherds kept him trapped against the fence for an hour before the Bradleys came home, and then Mike still had to explain why his baseball cards were buried in their doghouse.

To add to that satisfaction, Mom and Dad had forgiven me for leading Joel into a night of terror. I didn't even try explaining exactly who had terrified who. I knew better.

All told, being a hero wasn't bad. Lisa smiled at me again as Joel and I settled down across the aisle from her. I just wish being a hero could have lasted longer than the next fifteen minutes.

I was even pretty relaxed around Joel. Sharing a night in the woods and teaming with him to catch the spirits at camp had been good for us. I didn't even mind when Mom put me in charge of him during the church service.

Our church has babysitting during the adult services, and it was Mom and Dad's turn to volunteer, so Joel and I sat together on the pew and tried to listen carefully. I wanted to be on my best behavior, because Mrs. Henry was sitting beside us. She sometimes gets cross at me for accidently stepping on her cat's tail when I deliver her paper, even though I keep trying to explain that it won't move out of my way.

I was feeling especially proud just before the sermon when Pastor Stan talked about things that had happened to church people during the week. He started telling the congregation about the Cadets solving a mystery of sorts at Cadet camp. I looked over at Joel to see if he was equally proud.

My heart sank. He was playing with a tiny mouse.

"Joel—" I hissed.

"From camp," he breathed.

What could I do? I reached over and took it from him, hoping

Mrs. Henry wouldn't notice. The mouse fit into my hand with only its head sticking out and it rested happily. Only Joel could have tamed a mouse so well.

Joel calmly reached into his jacket pocket and took out another mouse. Why it has to be my kid brother who can perform miracles with animals, I'll never know.

"Joel—" I hissed again.

He shrugged crossly and handed it to me. I held the mouse in my other hand. It was going to be a long, long church service.

Mrs. Henry nudged me. I kept my hands out of sight.

She cooed, "That was wonderful what you and Joel did. I already heard it from three different people." I squirmed. She dug into her purse. Great. Even with empty hands, I wasn't fond of her peppermints. She always left them loose in her purse and they were usually purple with lint.

She nudged me again and offered me one. I shook my head.

"Take one," she whispered. "You deserve it."

I shook my head again. She frowned, then noticed my hands were tucked beneath the pew.

Mrs. Henry has told me a hundred times about how she raised her children without any nonsense. She didn't even ask what I had in my hands. She reached down and pulled both my hands out from under the pew.

The mouse gave a friendly blink.

For someone who raised children without any nonsense, Mrs. Henry wasn't very brave. She screeched in fright and slapped my hands, knocking the mice loose. A mouse darted onto her lap.

Mrs. Henry screeched again and stood up, shaking her dress and jumping wildly. Both mice took off and scooted in different directions. It was easy to tell where they went. Every time one scurried past another pew, someone else jumped and screeched.

I shook my head. *Explain this one to parents,* I thought. Joel stayed mad at me for a week for letting his mice get away.

SIGMUND BROUWER was born in 1959 to Dutch immigrant parents in Red Deer, Alberta, Canada. For many years after high school graduation he seemed incapable of holding a steady job, despite (or because of) two separate university degrees.

From slaughterhouse butchering to heavy-duty truck driving to semi-pro hockey, he ardently pursued any type of work that did not lead to becoming a lawyer, his mother's fondest dream.

After years of traveling, to the relief of his warm and loving Christian family, he returned home and has since donned a cloak of respectability as a former senior editor of NATIONAL RACQUETBALL, an international magazine published from Florida, as a current publisher of various local weekly magazines, and as writing instructor at the local college.

He now spends much of his writing time in conference with Ricky and Joel Kidd. Many of the resulting short stories with them and the rest of the Accidental Detectives have appeared in various magazines in the United States, Canada, and Australia.

Sigmund has no intention of leaving his hometown again, except, of course, to travel.

... Our silence was comfortable ... ... few minutes as all of us were lost in our thoughts. Then Mike began restlessly strumming his fingers on the empty cookie package.

"You're getting pretty good at that, Mike," I said. In school sometimes, we strum our fingers on the desks and see who can do it the fastest, loudest, and longest.

"Pretty good at what?"

"You know. Strumming with your fingers."

"Oh-oh," he said. "I thought that was you strumming on the flashlight."

"Knock if off, Guys," Ralphy warned. "You know I throw up if I get too scared."

There was nothing to knock off. The strumming got louder and suddenly all of us knew one thing. *It was a horse.*

We pushed ourselves into the shadow of the rock.

Across the gorge, outlined sharply against the moon, we saw a rider on a horse. Even from that distance, we could see long hair flowing back from the rider as she moved at full gallop!

The horse and rider faded into shadows. Then the drumming of hooves stopped. There was a long silence. Then we heard a clattering as the horse began to pick its way down into the gorge.

"No horse can do that," I whispered. "Those cliffs are too steep."

"That horse can," Mike hissed in return. "And it sounds like it's headed this way."

... in **PHANTOM OUTLAW AT WOLF CREEK**